Richard Gordon was born in 1921. He ⸋
on to work as an anaesthetist at St Bart⸋
ship's surgeon. As obituary-writer for ⸋
inspired to take up writing full time an⸋
embark on his 'Doctor' series. This proved incredibly successful ⸋⸋
subsequently adapted into a long-running television series.

Richard Gordon has produced numerous novels and writings all
characterised by his comic tone and remarkable powers of observation. His
Great Medical Mysteries and *Great Medical Discoveries* concern the stranger
aspects of the medical profession whilst his *The Private Life of...* series takes a
deeper look at individual figures within their specific medical and
historical setting. Although an incredibly versatile writer, he will,
however, probably always be best known for his creation of the hilarious
'Doctor' series.

Doctor on the Ball

Richard Gordon

This edition published in 2001 by House of Stratus, an imprint of Stratus Holdings plc, 24c Old Burlington Street, London, W1X 1RL, UK.

www.houseofstratus.com

Typeset, printed and bound by House of Stratus.

A catalogue record for this book is available from the British Library.

ISBN 1-84232-520-5

1

For twenty-five years have I practised in Churchford, a pleasant and prosperous old market town in Kent, now populated largely by middle-class commuters obsessed with their weight. I have steadfastly observed them in the nude, wrestled with their indigestion, insomnia, allergies, phobias, depressions, bronchitis, sexual fantasies and aversion to relatives. I have prescribed sufficient tranquillizers to soothe the tormented devils of Hell, enough laxatives to move the bowels of the earth, and have spread with the pill more carefree enjoyment than Horizon Holidays.

I started single-handed from the Victorian villa where we live, the medical equivalent of the corner shopkeeper or jobbing builder. Now I have an architect-designed surgery and three partners to share the pains of my profession, which grotesquely combines the servitude of a lackey with the authority of a saint, the tenderness of a bride with the steeliness of an assassin, scholarship with squalor, sorcery with science, and handicraft with hocus-pocus.

After a quarter of a century, I am often bored with it. Patients are puzzled or shocked by this admission. But any customer, criminal, case, or confessor becomes much like another to the man who makes his livelihood disposing of him.

Luckily, the doctor enjoys one daily stimulant. What fascinating human conundrum might sit itself next on the consulting-room chair?

I have encountered some amazing cases, which I meant to write up for the education of my fellow-doctors in the learned journals, if only a lifetime of general practice had left me the time to do anything...

One bright, frosty January morning, spryly stepped into my custard-coloured consulting room Ernie Partridge, from *Mann's Estate*.

Or rather, Nigel Vaughan, the middle-aged actor who plays him in the TV serial about an estate created on the splendid principles of social engineering, which means the poor being obliged to live in unhomely flats tolerable only with the luxuries of the rich. The social mixture, polarizing like iron filings under a magnet, is irresistible to the class-obsessed British, who watch each week by countless millions.

Everyone is fascinated to see a famous actor close to, though they are generally as unremarkable out of action as performing seals. Nigel Vaughan was short, pink, plump, neatly prosperous in tweed jacket, canary pullover and suede boots. He differed from any commuting stockbroker at a weekend only by the lovely hair-do.

He was suffering from bellyache.

I began the well-worn clinical catechism. Where was the pain? Under the ribs, doctor. Severe? Oh, like a vice! Related to meals? Difficult to say, doctor, meals were irregular, the show's running through a bad patch. You see, we have rehearsals all week, shooting before a studio audience on Saturday night, and it goes out the next Tuesday. I asked, Had he any personal worries? He burst into tears.

'Dr Gordon,' he exclaimed, 'I am going to die.'

'Oh, tut tut,' I murmured soothingly. 'Oh, come, come. We mustn't jump to gloomy conclusions, must we?'

'But I *am*, doctor,' he insisted miserably. 'On January the thirty-first, to be exact.'

I wondered how the hell he knew, but said comfortingly, 'We haven't even made the diagnosis yet, have we? Lots of people suffer digestive trouble and live for years and years. It's the fifth commonest complaint family doctors see,' I consoled him. 'It comes between wax in the ears and backache. There's statistics to prove it.'

'But it's in the script, doctor,' he explained despairingly. 'They're writing me out. I've already been taken poorly. It was taped last Saturday, and it's on the air at seven thirty tonight. Next week, I'm worse. The week after I'm terrible. I haven't a chance. I've read the lines. I have only four more episodes to live.' He blew his nose on a tissue.

2

I frowned.

I have reached the age when my hairline can recede no farther, if my waistline enjoys infinite possibilities of advancement. My wife Sandra tuts as she untucks the seams of my favourite brown tweed suit, which she claims is more appropriate for the butts than the bedside. The cells of my brain have meanwhile been steadily degenerating at the rate of a million a week. Or perhaps day. Or possibly hour. So many have gone, I cannot remember. Its grip has lost its forceps' precision.

I slid my half-moons down my nose and stared at Nigel Vaughan. He stared back with the touching expression of patients towards their government-sponsored ministering angel – I am said by the more imaginative ones to resemble a cherub gone to seed.

'Now, wait a minute –' I sieved my thoughts. 'Let's get this straight. Look, Ernie Partridge is a terminal case, OK? And rotten luck to the poor fellow. But there is absolutely no reason for Nigel Vaughan to follow Ernie Partridge into an early grave,' I indicated, 'unless you are taking your profession with undue seriousness.'

He sat slowly shaking his head. 'It's all very well, you putting it like that, doctor. But I've been having these nasty pains and feeling utterly wretched since Hal Tibbs – that's our producer – revealed last month that Ernie was suffering from a fatal illness. Of course, Hal broke the news gently,' he conceded. 'He's a lovely man really. Pity he's such a bastard over the money.'

'But that's *Ernie* –'

Nigel Vaughan gulped. 'Hal took me out to lunch. He said he'd hardly the heart to tell me. They were all going to miss me terribly, it was just as if one of his own family had the skids on. I'll never forget it, as long as I live.'

'But *you* are Mr Vaughan –'

Suddenly he squared his shoulders, looked like the man between the wall and the firing squad. Actors can change their personality as easily as shuffling cards. 'I took the terrible news on the chin. I just said, If it's to be, Hal me old darling, it's to be. None of us can go on for ever. One day the very show itself may come to an end.'

'The patient is *Mr Partridge* –'

3

'Though God knows how I shall break it to the wife, I told him. Then Hal put down his balloon glass of brandy and took both my hands in his. It was a lovely gesture. As I often say, it takes a personal tragedy to show who your real friends are.'

'*Who—*'

'Hal advised me to set my affairs in order. No point in jibbing at the inevitable, is there? I phoned my agent that very afternoon. It's nice to know I'm leaving behind such wonderful people.'

He jumped. I had banged the desk.

'*Who does not exist!*'

'I know, I know,' he admitted wearily. 'But Ernie and Nigel have been one and the same bloke over ten years. When I go opening fêtes and that, I'm invited as Ernie Partridge. Everyone wants Ernie Partridge's autograph, not mine. It's not me nabbed for speeding in the papers, it's Ernie Partridge. *This* wasn't my *Life*, it was Ernie Partridge's. At that garden party in Buckingham Palace, the Queen was being gracious to Ernie Partridge. In pubs, people call me Ernie and ask after everyone in the show – not the cast, the real people, but the characters they're paid to perform. When the wife goes shopping, they call her Mrs Partridge and say how wonderful it must be having such a steady, loving hubby.'

He fell silent. I murmured something about the mysterious effect of mind on body. He asked sombrely, 'Do you know what a *Doppelgänger* is, doctor?'

'Yes, the ghost of someone who's still living.'

He nodded disconsolately. 'It can appear to other people while you're still walking about. Creepy. My trouble is not knowing exactly who's the spook – me or Ernie.'

'If you'll take off your jacket,' I directed, 'I'll examine both of you.'

Nothing abnormal.

Buttoning up his check shirt, Nigel Vaughan observed whimsically, 'You know, doctor, I've always had a longing to play Hamlet. I suppose most of us have in the profession, at one time or another. But I've had to take the parts that come along – "For we that live to please, must please to live," eh? Maybe you think I'm a bit past it? But the great Beerbohm Tree

4

played Hamlet at the Haymarket when he was over forty.' He sighed. 'Well, that's another ambition I've got to forget.'

I pointed out, 'But once you've escaped from the thespian treadmill of *Mann's Estate*, you'll be free to play Hamlet or Peter Pan or Charley's Aunt or whoever you feel like.'

His face lightened. 'So I will! It's somehow difficult to believe in life after Ernie's death.'

'Though I expect you'd run into the same trouble playing the Bard,' I pointed out. 'Most of his characters seem to exit on the point of a sword.'

I prescribed an antacid and warned him off chips and booze.

I could not observe the onset of Ernie Partridge's fatal illness that evening, through a meeting on GP–hospital relations at the Churchford General. I have complained for years that the consultants' gloriously trailed clouds of registrars and housemen only befog the GP about who is treating his patient. The surgery is efficient, but anonymous, like supermarket butchery. Perhaps communications will improve now my daughter Jilly is a surgical registrar there. (Against my advice. Hers is a forlorn career, poor dear. Despite the feminist explosion in the medical profession, surgery in the late twentieth century remains as predominantly a male activity as duelling in the early nineteenth.) She seems welcome at the General. Jilly is like her mother was, tall, blonde, with crisp features, and inclined to be bossy.

I thought deeply all week of Nigel Vaughan's case. Actors' emotions are their stock-in-trade, like the sportsman's eye or the athlete's wind. It is a strange job which demands a man memorize a conversation then deliver it in funny clothes as though passionate in every word. The actor who plays Othello must feel sulphurously jealous, Henry V enviably brave and Romeo dreadfully randy. (Though my friend Dr Lonelyhearts, who writes medical articles for the papers and moves in artistic circles, says that the greatest actors can deliver Caesar's funeral oration while working out their income tax.)

I decided that Nigel Vaughan's role was affecting his psychology as powerfully as vice versa. My diagnosis was the famous mental disease of *folie à deux*.

Let me explain this fascinating condition of second-hand madness, discovered by two French psychiatrists in 1873.

We all have days imagining that every policeman is watching us, every driver trying to murder us, and all the girls laughing behind our backs. Some people suffer permanent delusions of persecution – the neighbours, the Jesuits and Jews, the BBC are common culprits. These are trying to poison them, or accusing them of incest and murder, or bugging their homes and spying through the TV. Some sufferers in desperation move house, inevitably to find more persecutors awaiting. The mad ideas can spread to one, two or three perfectly sane relatives or friends, who believe as honestly as they that the Pope or the Editor of *The Times* is nightly pumping lethal gas through the bedroom curtains. The record for psychopathic fallout is twelve, a family in Taiwan, so deluded over non-existent mites crawling through their skins the poor things scratched themselves raw. The only oddity of Nigel Vaughan's condition was the two sufferers living inside his head like landlord and lodger.

A week later, I determined to join the countless millions watching *Mann's Estate*. I never do my share of the nation's television-watching (twenty hours a week, long enough to read aloud a quarter of the Bible). I switched on and settled down with my wife Sandra. She frequently supplies a clear, common-sense second opinion to my cases. She was once a staff nurse at my hospital of St Swithin's in the East End of London. Her tall figure remains amazingly slim, if the long fair hair once twined bewitchingly under her white cap has faded like the gold of a cornfield in the sunset. She is an incomparable helpmeet, though I sometimes allow myself the shameful fantasy of being a consultant neurosurgeon instead of a downtrodden GP had she come to me thirty years ago with more than two Liberty lawn dresses, a shelf of Penguins, a Teasmade and £26 4s 6d in the Post Office. As I advise our son Andy (in medical research), the best prescription for success in a medical career, as in all others, is to marry money.

The television scene was a tasteful lounge. My patient was staggering against the Parker-Knoll sofa and stumbling over the Habitat coffee table before clutching the Sanderson curtains lining the picture window. As he seized his belly and groaned like the creak of a graveyard gate, I observed with concern, 'You know, he really is a sick man.'

'A symptomatic spectacular,' Sandra agreed admiringly.

He retched noisily, endangering the white fitted carpet. I continued anxiously, 'I hope I haven't missed anything.'

'But it's only just started, Richard.'

'I mean, when I saw him last week,' I elucidated, as the poor fellow gripped his throat and howled like a dyspeptic dog. 'Supposing it wasn't simple indigestion? Suppose he's got a peptic ulcer, an acute gallbladder, cancer of the stomach? Any would fit his present state.' I felt sweat in my palms. 'Apart from the tragedy of unnecessary human suffering, I could have exposed myself to enormous damages for malpractice. You know what patients are like these days – get a diagnosis wrong, and you're in court quicker than going through a red light. Look at that!' I exclaimed in horror, as he tottered to a repro-Jacobean cocktail cabinet, grabbed a bottle of Scotch, upended it and gulped like a soccer player at half-time.

'Straight out of the bottle!' I complained crossly. 'When I strictly told him to knock it off. It's no wonder some patients take the short cut to the tomb, not following their doctor's advice. Frankly, I'm surprised and disappointed. He seemed such a responsible and stolid type.'

Sandra was staring at me. 'Are you mad?'

'What's the matter?' I asked shortly.

'You are looking at Ernie Partridge,' she pronounced slowly, nodding towards the screen. 'Who is an item of fiction, like King Kong.'

'Ah!'

'Your patient Nigel Vaughan,' she continued evenly, 'is traumatizing his stomach with nothing more horrible than cold tea.'

I gave a weak smile. 'How easy to get carried away by these soap operas,' I conceded. 'Don't you think the sinister quality of television is making fact and fiction indistinguishable? Nobody knows if they've really just watched the Bomb go off, or if it's special effects. The only difference in the fictional world is the acting being more lifelike.'

'I think you should fix with one of the partners and take a few days off,' said Sandra.

7

The programme ended with Ernie Partridge subsiding on the sofa, blood trickling from his mouth over his wife's new dress.

'Well, they're certainly making the point that he's rather off colour,' observed Sandra.

I was no longer concentrating. An icy flood of fear numbed my brain. Was this the first sign of presenile dementia?

2

Sandra had the right prescription. I needed a winter break.

Next lunchtime I visited our High Street travel agent's to flick through the brochures. As I leaned against the counter, entranced by near-naked girls lying in ecstasy on the rocks, a soft voice asked, 'Going somewhere?'

It was Dr Quaggy. Tall, spare and handsome, with smooth dark hair, steely moustache and expression of amiable authority, he resembled doctors in the pretty BUPA advertisements which make illness look like another of life's pleasures. He was Churchford's most successful GP, and like successful people everywhere was better at the politics of his occupation than its performance.

I mentioned a snatched weekend.

'I'd take a month.'

'A GP in midwinter? Impossible!'

'Don't you owe it to yourself, Richard?' he suggested in his quiet way. 'Your punishing workload is a byword in Churchford. We all marvel how you keep it up. Absolute martyrdom. Why not take a clear three months while you're at it, on one of these fascinating luxury cruises?'

I told him shortly, 'My partners wouldn't hear of it.'

He sighed. 'Neither would Bill Topping's. And look what happened. Fatal coronary only last Monday. Wasn't it the Frenchman Clemenceau who said, "Cemeteries are full of indispensable men"? Or you could go the whole hog and opt for early retirement.'

I said indignantly, 'The idea of retirement's never entered my head.'

He continued calmly, 'Perhaps, Richard, you'll thank me one day for installing it.' He leafed the seductive pages. 'There's some lovely places, just look – Marbella, Majorca, Malta. Pleasant, relaxed British people, plenty of parties, golf. Sandra could make a delightful home in one of those charming villas, which strike me as very reasonably priced. She loves the sun, doesn't she? After all, our pension's not to be sneezed at, and I'm sure you've done as well as me out of private practice; everyone calls you Churchford's most popular doctor.'

I changed the subject. 'Where are *you* off to?'

I'm after some ski brochures for my son Arnold. How's your own lad getting on?'

'Andy's landed a research job in the cardiac unit at St Swithin's,' I told him proudly.

'What splendid news! I'm sure he'll do wonderfully well. Even when they were students, Arnold reported him a high-flyer. Did you know that Arnold's doing his GP training? I must confess a sentimental wish that he could eventually practise here in Churchford. But of course, no immediate vacancies. Unless we have another premature death. Or a premature retirement? Much preferable!'

He gave a little laugh, like the whinny of the Trojan horse.

That week the flu epidemic hit Churchford. I had barely time to think of a rest. Nor of Nigel Vaughan, until he reappeared at the following Monday morning's surgery. I suspected queue-jumping, but Mrs Jenkins, our receptionist, smilingly assured me of everyone in the waiting room willingly postponing their appointments for so beloved a national invalid as Ernie Partridge.

He came sustained by Mrs Sophie Vaughan. She too was middle-aged and overweight, fair-haired and gold-braceleted, like any other prosperous local housewife chic from Robbins Modes (our fashionable High Street couturière).

'Why, you're looking *much* better,' I greeted him cheerfully, seating them facing the consulting-room desk. 'Much, much better! I'd say a complete transformation from the way you looked when I saw you last week. Yes, a different man,' I continued happily. 'I'm sure you think the same?' I invited from Sophie.

Nigel Vaughan was puzzled. 'But Dr Gordon, I haven't consulted you for nearly a fortnight. When you put me on the white pills, remember?'

'Yes, when I first examined you,' I agreed readily. 'But the next time I saw you, I must confess a little concern. Particularly as you did not seem to be heeding my warning against drink. Alcohol is a severe irritant to the stomach lining, you know, specially when swallowed neat. Indeed, straight out of the bottle – '

'But doctor! That was Ernie Partridge you were watching knocking back the booze.'

I aligned my thoughts.

'Just my little joke,' I said feebly. 'TV can seriously damage your health.'

'I'm still having the pangs, doctor,' he declared, looking miserable again. 'Real ones, not electronic. Even though Sophie's making me special things like boiled fish and coddled eggs, aren't you dear? As for the drink, I haven't touched a drop. Not that I've ever indulged in much more than a sherry. Though it's funny,' he mused, 'all doctors seem to think that all actors, whatever's wrong with them, have also got cirrhosis of the liver as a matter of course.'

'Come and see the show being recorded on Saturday,' invited Sophie eagerly. 'After all, the studios aren't far away.'

Off the London to Churchford motorway stood a cluster of buildings like aircraft hangars, which once produced epics of the British cinema, largely starring Alec Guinness.

'You might find the studio audience a bit dull, being busloads of OAPs,' Nigel added doubtfully. 'And maybe you'd think the warm-up man a bit basic.'

'You should have watched last week's show,' Sophie continued enthusiastically. 'Sensational!'

'As you know, I'm a pillar of respectability on the Estate,' Nigel explained more warmly. 'The father figure, everyone turning to me with their problems, sex, drink, money, relatives, all that. I'm above all the little squabbles, deceits, disloyalties inevitable in any community.'

'Like a good GP?' I suggested.

He nodded. 'That's right. But we're all human, aren't we? And now it's suddenly come out,' he confessed solemnly. 'I have put a flighty young secretary with child.'

'Oh, dear,' I muttered.

'But I am standing by him, doctor,' Sophie asserted quietly. 'What is it but the lapse of any man recapturing his youth? No, it shall make no difference to our marriage,' she said determinedly. 'None whatever. *That* is something based on mutual affection and trust. And on understanding the little frailties of those who love us.'

'Particularly,' Nigel added, rubbing the canary pullover, 'in view of my delicate state of health.'

'I must say, I admire your tolerant attitude,' I told her sympathetically. 'As you can guess, this is a problem which comes before us doctors fairly regularly. How much more sensible you are than many other wives — particularly young, inexperienced ones, to whom marriage is ridiculously romantic.'

He declared firmly, 'Marriage is as practical as any other job of work in your life.'

'And our love burns as steadfastly as a lighthouse on a rock, whatever the storms and tides that battle against it,' she confirmed.

'Very nicely put, both of you.'

'It's in the script,' said Nigel.

I drilled my thoughts. 'Wait a minute!' I exclaimed. 'It's not you, it's Ernie having the little bastard.'

'Oh, doctor!' Sophie gave a slow smile. 'It's so confusing, really. As Nigel is Ernie to everyone, even the neighbours, even the vicar when he comes to call, so I'm Mrs Partridge. I mean, it stands to reason, doesn't it? I'm his lawful wedded wife.'

'Quite,' I said confusedly. 'Quite, quite.'

She sighed deeply. 'Sometimes I wonder if we really live inside our lovely timbered home or inside everyone's TV set.'

'Keep on taking the tablets,' I suggested hastily, deciding the problems of Nigel's dyspepsia simpler than those of Ernie's paternity. 'Though if the pain persists, perhaps we'd better toddle along to the General for an X-ray.'

'Any time you like, doctor, before January the thirty-first. I thought I'd take a short holiday once I'm dead.'

I have really no need to buy newspapers. A glance round my waiting patients provides all Fleet Street's headlines. That Wednesday, most declaimed ERNIE'S SHAME! After surgery, I opened a discarded tabloid and read its sentimental and scandalized story of the sensationally ill-conceived child. What will Mrs Ernie do? the paper asked agitatedly. Will she stand by him? Is Ernie *really* dying? In that unfortunate event, the article suggested, will she adopt the baby to perpetuate Ernie's name for posterity, in episodes stretching into infinity?

I turned to Mrs Jenkins, tidying her desk. I said smugly, 'She *will* stand by him.'

'Doctor?'

I held up the newspaper. 'Ernie's wife. She won't let this paternity business destroy their marriage, which is as sound as a lighthouse on a rock. She told me exactly that, here in the surgery last Monday.'

Mrs Jenkins pursed her lips and drummed them with her fingertips.

'Doctor…I may be thick, but…wasn't it the actor and his wife you were treating?'

I gave a little laugh. 'Just pulling your leg,' I pretended.

My case had become more serious than my patient's. His *folie à deux* had spread like measles to *folie à trois*. Or was I just another case in an epidemic of *folie à tous* sweeping the country, worse than the itching Taiwanese?

Or was it just another illustration that all the world's a stage? People took me for a doctor because I acted like a doctor. Judges, bishops and soccer hooligans all gave the performances expected by their public. The world picked its leaders because they looked statesmanlike on television, which is like buying the poke as well as the pig. If everyone thought of Nigel Vaughan as Ernie Partridge, who imagined Boris Karloff without rivets in his neck?

I sombrely determined on a word with Ollie Scuttle, the psychiatrist at Churchford General Hospital, if I saw him in the golf club on Sunday.

As I strolled into the club bar after my morning round, I found myself facing Hal Tibbs.

I had forgotten he was a member. He lived near the studios in a floodlit Elizabethan house with a swimming pool, and had an electric golf buggy. He played terrible golf, but our community cherished him as a curiosity. The Nottingham Miners' Club probably thought the same about D H Lawrence.

I went straight to the point.

'I say, it's a bit hard, isn't it? Suddenly sacking a fine actor like Nigel Vaughan. After ten years in your show, too.'

Hal Tibbs grinned over his Buck's fizz. He was a large man with a complexion like smoked salmon and an eye always glancing over your shoulder for someone more interesting. 'I've no complaints about the publicity, doc, and I don't think he has.'

I demurred. 'The publicity can't be helped, but the judgement does seem a little severe on the poor fellow.'

Hal Tibbs looked wary. 'What do you know that the papers don't?'

'Nothing,' I admitted, 'but losing your job these days seems a tough price for a little bit of scandal.'

His eyebrows rose. 'Scandal?'

'Putting your secretary in pod, of course. Happen to anyone in a moment's aberration. Businessmen, MPs, Cabinet ministers, even doctors, always getting away with it. I'd have thought you were more broadminded in the world of entertainment. Oh, I know some tiresome people think television should be a branch of the Church of England, but I'm certain his millions of fans would be only too delighted if the girl ended up with quins.'

He stared. 'You taking the mickey?'

'No, but as an ordinary, decent, tolerant member of the public, I'd like to put in a good –'

I stopped.

He laughed. 'You've been watching too much TV, doc. Bad for the eyes, isn't it? Turns 'em square. Have a drink.'

I silently took a Glenfiddich in a numb grasp. My condition was becoming desperate.

Hal Tibbs explained amiably, 'It's hardly top secret in the business that we're writing Nigel out because we've a big American actor coming in, and we can't afford both. Simple as that. It's all in the papers next week. But don't cry for Nigel, some West End management's putting him into a season of *Hamlet*. Can't lose, can they? The viewers would queue to see him as the back legs of a pantomime horse. For a couple of months, until they forget all about him, of course,' he ended casually.

I went home shaken to Sunday lunch. Sandra said I had better make it a week off.

Andy appeared that evening from London. He resembles me, except for the infuriating, insolent lissomness of youth. He drinks single malt whisky, for which I have transmitted the appreciative gene. His research into coronary artery disease retains him in the wards of St Swithin's, where Jilly and myself trained as doctors, also their grandfather and two uncles, one who was struck off but married the girl.

Andy greeted me, 'I hear you're retiring, Dad?'

I frowned. 'Whatever gave you that outlandish notion?'

'I met Arnold Quaggy at the St Swithin's reunion last night – he's the same bumptious little creep. Apparently, you'd told his old man you were quitting this year for Marbella. I hope you'll invite me for my holidays?'

'Outrageous!' I exclaimed angrily. 'It was Quaggy trying to sell the idea to me in a travel bureau.'

'Ah, that explains it. Arnold was telling everyone cockily about his father fixing it with the Family Practitioner Committee he'd get your job.'

I was horrified. 'God forbid! They'd snake their way into all the local committees, call the tune for general practice in Churchford, and between them grab all the private patients.'

'That's the idea,' assessed Andy calmly.

Nigel Vaughan was at Monday morning's surgery. The stomach was worse. He rubbed the canary pullover harder than ever. He couldn't eat, couldn't sleep, barely think. It was dreadfully worrying, because he must be in peak form for Saturday's recording of the big episode when he died.

'I'll give you an urgent letter for a private consultation with Dr Gravelston,' I told him, 'who is the big star of the stomach scene.'

'Sooner the better, doctor,' he said unhappily. 'I can't face another night like last. I really felt I was about to expire before my time. Which would be a terrible pity, because my death will be the performance of my life.'

'Quite,' I said. 'Quite, quite.'

I spent the day worrying if I had referred to old Gravelston Mr N Vaughan or Mr E Partridge.

During next morning's surgery Mrs Jenkins announced agitatedly that she had a raving maniac on the line. It was Hal Tibbs.

'Doc? Got you!' he exclaimed excitedly. 'What's the matter with Nigel?'

I hesitated. 'I cannot discuss my patients,' I said stiffly.

'I know he's in hospital,' Hal snapped impatiently. 'They said at his home Sophie'd just taken him in. I've got to get hold of him. It's a matter of life and death.'

I calmed him down. 'It's only for an X-ray. He'll be back by lunchtime.'

'Thank God!' cried Hal Tibbs. 'You see, he isn't going to die after all.'

'Oh, there's no question of that,' I reassured him quickly. 'It's only a routine investigation.'

'I mean on Saturday night. The big American actor's pulled out. We're rewriting the episode so he's saved by the miracles of modern medicine. Next week he'll be feeling absolutely fine. But he's got to learn the lines by tomorrow morning.'

'Delighted to hear it!' I said heartily. 'I'll see he gets the good news straight away. He'll need cheering up, he's probably in the middle of a barium meal.'

Our red-brick, slate-roofed, Gothic-porticoed, bow-windowed and finger-chimneyed villa in Foxglove Lane resembles the Welsh chapels, Highland railway halts and seaside boarding houses created by the freely interchangeable Victorian architectural flair. I had bought it twenty-five years ago, to run my one-man practice with the ingenuity, toil and watchfulness of Robinson Crusoe. We have been intending to move for years, but I cannot tolerate the conversation of house agents. We have withdrawn like England's dukes to a corner of our encumbering residence, comfortable enough amid amiably threadbare furniture and dull unmeddlesome decorations. A kitchen large enough to feed fecund Victorian families delightfully catches the sun at breakfast, the following morning interrupted by our front doorbell. In the drive stood Nigel and Sophie Vaughan, on the way to the studios in their Mercedes.

'Doctor –'

Nigel clasped my hand and stared silently into my eyes. I returned the glance solemnly.

'I have come to say only half a dozen words,' he continued quietly. 'Which mean more than all others ever written in the world. Thank you for saving my life.'

I muttered, 'I was only doing my job.'

'So my guardian angel might have said.' He wiped his eyes with the sleeve of his vicuña overcoat. 'Last night,' he said reverently, 'the wife and I got on our knees and offered up a little prayer for you.'

I felt a lump in my throat.

'That you may live long to continue your wonderful good work in an undeserving world,' explained Sophie softly.

He put his hand in his overcoat pocket. He produced a wristwatch. 'From an eternally grateful patient.'

'It's Swiss, not Jap,' said Sophie.

I mumbled brokenly.

They entered their car. They waved. They drove down the drive, stopped, and waved again. They went off into the winter sunrise.

I slowly shut the front door.

'Your bacon's getting cold, Richard,' called Sandra from the kitchen. 'Who was it?'

'Nigel Vaughan,' I replied simply. 'He brought me this. For snatching him from the grave.'

She frowned. 'But you said the barium meal was negative. There was no need to snatch him from anywhere.'

I clasped my brow. 'Sandra –'

'Yes?'

'Can you still get into last year's swimsuit?'

'I should hope so.'

'Ring Wintersun Travel. I'm taking my annual holiday.'

'Whoever's life we saved between us, doc,' reflected Hal Tibbs when I next met him at the golf club, 'at least we did the world a favour. We stopped poor old Nigel ever playing Hamlet.'

3

When I arrived in Churchford twenty-five years ago, the Victorian villas like ours had delightful gardens with tennis courts, which all summer emitted a cheerful *ping* and cries of 'Sorry, partner!'

Then they built houses on the tennis courts. Next, they built houses on the gardens of those houses, filling in the serving courts. Now, whole families are accommodated in the sidelines.

When us quartet of single-handed doctors combined as sensibly as four handymen starting their own repairs business, the increased population justified our custom-built single-storey surgery a mile from my home in Chaucer Way, shopping street of the 1930s developers' dream – convenient for station, fast trains to London – of living in *rus* and working in *urbe*. Like most dreams, this faded to the scruffy commonplace. Its tatty semis provide a third of our patients, the old middle class in the new human hutches a half, the remaining sixth our enviable émigrés, the classless new rich with lovely homes, a Merc and a Spanish girl.

Our waiting room has a functional decor, mustard-coloured walls enlivened with cheery posters warning the population on the dangers of smoking and of incautious eating, sex and stepping off pavements. The furniture enjoys the comfortless durability of bus seats, the plastic underfoot as obdurate to our patients as the marbled floors of St Peter's to its pilgrims. It is warm, clean and odourless, its stereotyped bleakness accepted by the public in trouble with the equally nervous resignation it affords courts of justice.

Our four consulting rooms are small, with a couch and our everyday tools for taking blood pressure and looking into convenient orifices. We have a room of grey metal filing cabinets like the bowels of a warship, lots of loos, and of course somewhere to make the tea.

For ten years Mrs Jenkins our receptionist has discharged the job of secretary, filing clerk, checkout girl, public relations officer, tea lady, diplomat, first-aider, nanny, agony aunt and bodyguard, with the efficiency of Jeeves, Florence Nightingale, Portia and the Three Musketeers.

I suspected her keen cutting edge was blunting one breezy mid-February morning, when I demanded, 'Where were my last two patients' cards?'

'You're sitting on them. I left them on your chair, because you keep losing things in the muddle on your desk.'

'Of course it isn't a muddle. No more than the human interior. I know exactly where everything is. You haven't brought my coffee.'

'You *are* in a filthy temper this morning. You've drunk it.'

'Nonsense.'

'What's that empty cup, then? Under the path forms.'

'I've so many important things on my mind,' I muttered. 'This my final patient? Where's his card?'

'Can't find it.' Mrs Jenkins is small, dark and fiery-eyed.

'Really! What's his name, then?'

'Don't know.'

'Look here, you have absolutely no excuse –'

'I have. It's a case of loss of memory.'

'Oh. I see. Well. Send him in.'

A slight, brown-haired, neat man in his thirties, wearing a carefully kept blue suit, plain shirt, nondescript tie and shining black shoes. He entered with an air of quiet desperation.

'You've got to help me, doctor.'

'So we don't know who we are, then?' I commiserated, sitting him down. 'For how long haven't we known? Or have we forgotten?'

'It's like this, doctor,' he explained. 'I found myself walking down the street, outside Marks and Spencer's. I don't know how I got there. I didn't know who I was. Nasty turn, it gave me. I seemed to be in a nice place –

trees, tea rooms, Green Line bus stops, and that. I asked someone the name, pretending I'd caught the wrong bus. Then I discovered this in my pocket.'

A small blue diary, sold by every stationer's at Christmas. 'Only thing filled in was doctor's phone number. So I found a callbox and asked your lady outside for the address. Also, it seems I am blood group 0, Rh positive.'

'I've some good news.'

'Oh, yes?'

'I've never set eyes on you before. So you're perfectly healthy.'

But he seemed disinclined to look on the bright side.

'Try and remember – had you arrived in Churchford by car?'

'I might have descended from Heaven,' he replied bemusedly.

'Well, an attack of amnesia won't excuse even a chariot of fire left at a meter, not with our fearsome parking women.'

He frowned. 'A meter? A *parking* meter? Yes, it seems to mean something...'

I too needed to remember. What was the psychology of amnesia? Had I treated a case before? I had completely forgotten. I recalled something about amnesia providing escape from difficult circumstances.

'Any personal problems?' I inquired. 'Pockets contain a summons to appear at the Old Bailey? Or a letter regretting that your firm must dispense with your valuable services? Something in capitals saying the photos will be handed over for five grand in used tenners? Your own suicide note?' I suggested hopefully.

'Nothing except half a packet of mints and a few quid.'

'We'd better phone the police,' I decided. 'At this moment, they've probably got frogmen looking everywhere for you in the local reservoir.'

He moved uneasily in his chair. 'I'd prefer not getting involved with the police, if you don't mind.'

'Oh? On the run?'

'I've a vague feeling of guilt about something,' he admitted. 'Maybe I left a loving wife and lots of little ones somewhere? This was tucked in the lining of my jacket.'

He passed a cracked photograph of a fat grinning blonde in a minute bikini lying on a beach under a sign saying CERVEZA.

I exclaimed, 'Your case is cured.'

He jerked with relief.

'You are Mr Ackroid.'

'Go on?'

'This is Mrs Ackroid.'

'Coo.'

'I'd recognize her laparotomy scar anywhere.' I buzzed Mrs Jenkins to get the Ackroid number. 'Mrs Ackroid? This is Dr Gordon. Good morning. I have some important news for you.'

'Oh, yes?'

'Your hubby will be home in ten minutes.'

'Christ! I haven't seen the bugger for three years.'

I felt disconcerted, as if the returning Argonauts were told to stuff the Golden Fleece.

'What's he been up to?' she demanded sharply.

I broke the news. 'I'm afraid that he's suffering from an attack of loss of memory.'

'Oh, I wouldn't put nothing past him.'

'Would you care to speak to your husband?'

'Not much point, is there? If he doesn't remember who I am.'

'Obviously I must restore him to base. And I feel sure, Mrs Ackroid, that his memory will come flooding back once joyously reunited with yourself. Such patients respond excellently to loving and orderly environment.'

'I don't know how I shall manage, I really don't, it's been a terrible day already, what with the washing machine.'

'You'll have plenty to talk about,' I consoled her. 'A lot must have happened in three years.'

'Bloody right, it has. Well, I suppose somebody's got to take him in.'

'An admirable sense of family responsibility,' I congratulated her. 'Put on your best dress.' I replaced the telephone. 'You can toddle along home now, Mr Ackroid.'

'I've forgotten where it is.'

'Ah! I'll drop you on my way to visit the St Boniface Twilight Home.'

Mr Ackroid seemed to be steadily losing enthusiasm. He silently collected his dark overcoat from the waiting room. He sat sullenly in the car as I drove towards Rosemary Road, beyond the railway line. It started snowing.

'Aren't you excited at the prospect of being reunited with your dear ones?' I inquired.

'I've a feeling I've got problems.'

'But now you've a lovely wife to help you forget them.'

'Forgetting is something I'd like to forget about,' he remarked gloomily, as I stopped at the gate of a mock Tudor semi-det.

The front door opened.

'Christ!' screeched Mrs Ackroid. '*That* ain't my bleeding husband. It's Mr Hemmings.'

She grabbed his sleeve, pulled him across the tiny front garden, hauled him inside and slammed the door.

What to do? My professional duty was discharged. I shrugged. I drove off. It would clearly be best to let them sort it all out themselves.

Mrs Jenkins remarked in my consulting room between patients the following Monday morning, 'I'm surprised that you were fooled by the shifty sort who pretended he'd lost his memory.'

I said firmly, 'It was a genuine case of amnesia. Which is a form of psychological hysteria, like sleepwalking, fits of the shakes, creepy-crawly feelings up the skin, even imaginary deafness and blindness,' I educated her. 'All in the mind, with no bodily cause and causing no bodily harm. Always happening to soldiers in battles, and I believe the Army puts them in the glasshouse for losing their memory like any other item of their equipment. My patient is probably reacting to a tricky marital situation. I can only speculate.'

'Not for long. Mrs Ackroid's outside.'

Mrs Ackroid took the patient's chair, beginning anxiously, 'There's something queer about my Charlie. That's Mr Hemmings.'

'Are you embroidering the rich tapestry of his life as you gather the stray strands of memory?' I inquired.

'No, we're not.'

'But surely he can recall his job? His favourite viewing? His National Insurance number?'

'He can't remember nothing. He just wanders round the house staring out of the window and heaving deep sighs and saying he's probably done something awful, maybe murder, maybe fiddling the social security, it gets on your nerves.'

'Exaggerated feelings of guilt and self-reproach are common in depressed patients,' I reassured her.

'There's other things.' She leaned forward. 'Charlie shouldn't have been at home anyway, last weekend. He works on North Sea oil, you see. So he gets back only every other one, sometimes not even that when they're busy after striking a gusher, or whatever. I'm worried they're missing him. I mean, I get good money at the burger bar, but he doesn't want to risk the sack, every little helps these days, doesn't it?'

'Put the point to him. He seems an admirably sensible man.'

'He's ever so nice when he's sane,' she said fondly. 'And a real home bird. I often say of a Saturday let's go down the pub, but he says, I would rather sit viewing by the fire alone with you, my darling, in pubs you never know who you're going to meet.' She was suddenly despairing. 'I just don't know how to handle him, doctor, especially as I'm in the middle of redecorating the bathroom and toilet.'

'Ignore his mood, Mrs Ackroid,' I instructed her. 'My best advice is to be loving.'

'Oh, he hasn't forgotten anything about *that*, believe you me. You think Charlie's one of the quiet sort? But once he gets going, honest, if you made a video of it we'd be run in for hard porn.' She wriggled her pelvis reminiscently in the chair.

At evening surgery that Monday Mrs Jenkins announced, 'The man you gave to Mrs Ackroid is in the waiting room. Why don't you call the police?'

I demanded crossly, 'Surely you can tell the difference between the clinical and the crooked?'

'In this job you learn to spot the phoneys quicker than a computer spots stolen credit cards,' she told me crisply. 'That's why I think you're being conned like a bumpkin in Soho.'

'Kindly send in my patient,' I ordered icily.

Mrs Jenkins had been overdoing it. I must suggest to my partners that she enjoy a rest.

Charlie started awkwardly, 'I've got a bit of a confession to make, doctor. I hadn't lost my memory outside Marks and Spencer's. It happened earlier that morning. Shall I go on?'

'Please,' I invited.

'It had already gone when I woke up. I didn't know where I was. I suppose we all get that panicky feeling from time to time, away from home.'

'I have it inevitably in hotels, particularly as all the bedrooms these days look exactly the same.'

'So I screwed up my eyes and said, "It's all right, me old chum, another moment and everything will come back." But it didn't. I opened them again. I was in a small room with big pink roses on the wallpaper, a scruffy carpet and bright pink curtains keeping out the sunlight. Worse, I didn't know *who* I was. I was in a bed with a pink muslin canopy draped over the top end. I turned, and found myself six inches from a pink-faced ginger-headed girl, with her eyes shut and her mouth wide open, who I didn't know from Eve. She didn't have a fig leaf, neither.'

'Disconcerting,' I sympathized.

'Before I could react to this, without opening her eyes or, I think, closing her mouth, she grabbed me by what you doctors call the organs.'

'Do go on.'

'Well, what was I to do? Not much choice, really. So I did. I mean, wouldn't you?'

'I cannot answer hypothetical questions, as the politicians say on television.'

'She didn't even open her eyes till afterwards, when she said, "How's your poor head, Fred?" Come to think of it, I had quite a headache. She said, "I'm sure he didn't really mean to duff you up, he was only showing off." I asked, "What happened?" She said, "When he hit you, you banged your head against the lounge doorpost and passed out. I carried you up to bed. Kevin's ashamed of himself this morning, I shouldn't wonder." "Who's Kevin?" I asked. "Oh, come on," she said. "My husband, of course."'

'Intriguing.'

'Then I heard a creak outside the bedroom. There were other people in the house, see? Perhaps the husband? I thought. She leaped out of bed and started putting on her bra and pants warming on the electric heater, then pulled back the curtains and said, "You'd think it was spring," slipped into a pink satin housecoat and left me. Through the window I found rows of council houses, all with their back gardens and washing lines. I began to notice a nice smell of frying bacon. Lying on the tatty dressing table was a plugged-in electric razor, so I had a quick shave, put on this very suit, and went downstairs. The girl was at the kitchen table with a fat woman who must have been her mum, and a thin bloke smoking a hand-rolled and reading the *Sun*.'

'You are obviously one of the family,' I observed encouragingly.

Charlie – or Fred – nodded. 'Mum asked, "How's your head?" and shovelled me a plate of bacon, fried eggs, sausages and fried bread. "That Kevin will find himself inside again quicker than you can say the Sweeney Todd," she said. And the old boy said, without looking up from the *Sun*, "They oughter bring back the rope." And the girl said, "Fred, I didn't know Kevin was getting out yesterday, honest I didn't, I'd got it wrong about his remission." I said – a bit anxiously – "Is he upstairs?" and she said, "What, have that perverted villain in the house, you must be joking, he could sleep on a park bench as far as I'm concerned, though I suppose he'll be back some time, after all he is my husband, and maybe he'll still feel a bit sore about finding you here, Fred dearest, I should take a walk."'

'A prudent suggestion, perhaps.'

'So I put on my overcoat as it seemed a chilly time of year, and at the front door the old boy tucked the *Sun* under his arm and said, "I'd like it today." I said, "What today?" and he said, "That thump last night make you lose your memory, or something? The money." "Ah, the money," I said. He said, "The bloke what I owe it to is turning nasty. I mean, Fred, you been getting your knees under the table, living off the fat of the land, frozen duck, I ask you, about time you contributed to the household expenses, not to mention you having a slice of our Norma for long enough. You can't be short of a bob, with this market research job what gets you running round the country for weeks on end, but if you're feeling a bit doubtful about the donation maybe I'll tell Kevin a few things what I overhear between you and our Norma through the bedroom wall? These houses are a proper disgrace the way they're jerry built, someone made a packet out of it somewhere, believe you me." '

He paused. I placed my fingertips together. The sparseness of my comments indicated only the busyness of my brain.

'The old boy added in a nasty way, "Might make Kevin want to finish off last night's job, then?" So I started walking pretty smartish, anywhere to get away, along those roads of exactly the same houses, till I found myself in a busy shopping street and felt in my pockets and rang you up.'

'Nothing you have just told me ever happened.'

'But doctor! It's as vivid as you are sitting there, all pink with your half-moon glasses.'

'There is a lovely poem by the late Walter De la Mare, which proclaims, *Memory — that strange deceiver! Who can trust her? How believe her?* You lost your memory, certainly. I estimate some time before last weekend. Possibly you cracked under the strain of the North Sea. It must be dreadfully uncomfortable and draughty. But the rest is *pure hallucination*,' I told him impressively. 'Hallucinations are not uncommon concomitants of any psychological disturbance. This remarkably deprived family you have described will shortly fly forgotten as a dream dies at the opening day, as the Hymn Book puts it.'

With unaccustomed animation, he jumped up and shook my hand.

I beamed. 'You just go back living happily with Mrs Ackroid, who I know greatly appreciates you.'

How rare is the satisfaction in general practice of successfully treating single-handed an intricate and unusual case! Even Mrs Jenkins had to say grudgingly, 'He looked a lot happier when he left.'

'After twenty-five years as a GP, I may have acquired nothing but a profound knowledge of human nature,' I told her modestly.

I believe I heard her mutter, 'Or of single malt whiskies.' Perhaps it was time we bettered an offer of a rest with one of retirement. Perhaps I should refer her to Dr Quaggy.

When I got home I opened a bottle of Talisker.

'Any interesting cases, darling?' asked Sandra.

'Oh, the usual domestic difficulties,' I told her.

4

It is remarkable in medicine how one rare case brings another. See a case of fibrocystic disease, which occurs in only one of 2000 people, and another suspected case appears at the next surgery. Thursday morning produced Mrs Wilberforce. She is dark, snub-nosed, pleasant, with two young children, a part-time schoolteacher with asthma. She always retains the coolness of standing chalk-in-hand at the blackboard.

'Doctor, I have a personal problem' she began. 'I know it's not really your job, but I'd prefer putting it to you.'

'Please do,' I invited. 'Everyone else does.'

She bit her full lower lip. 'My husband seems to be making us into a one-parent family.'

'Tut,' I sympathized.

'As perhaps you know, my Herbert is a self-employed do-it-yourself double-glazing salesman. So he's not at home weekends. That's the only time he can be sure of finding people in their own home and persuade them to double-glaze it.'

I acknowledged the logic.

'But this week he hasn't put in his usual appearance Monday–Friday.'

I suggested at once, 'He's wandering about the country suffering loss of memory. We doctors see many such cases.'

'I can't imagine it,' she said doubtfully. 'Herbert's never had a day's illness in his life, physical, mental or imaginary.'

'Yes, I can't recall ever setting eyes on your husband,' I agreed. 'Have you suffered any domestic difficulties that he might wish to escape from?'

'Funny you should say that, doctor.' She was impressed. 'I think it's all to do with another woman.'

'Oh? Why?'

'Long blonde hairs.'

'On his collar?'

'In his Y-fronts.'

'Ah.'

'Actually, we had a blazing row about it last Friday morning, and I haven't seen him since.'

'Why not inform the police? They'll increase their list of missing persons by one.'

'I don't think Herbert would care for that at all,' she objected. 'Not finding himself in the company of dropouts, drug addicts and such. Rather a snobbish person, my Herbert. Keeps very much to himself. It's quite a job getting him out of the house. I often say when I come home from work at the Beowulf Comprehensive, how about leaving Tim and Anna with Gran and having a Chinky meal at the Ho Ho Ho!, but he always says, what's wrong with their takeaway, you only get people staring at you in restaurants.'

I could suggest only an advert in the papers on the lines Come Home All Is Forgiven. I added, 'I'll let you know at once if he phones me. Patients who lose their memory generally find their doctor's telephone number in their diaries and ring for help. How's the asthma? Good! Not much of it about this time of the year.'

The week passed without the reappearance of Charlie-Fred. I assumed he was busily digging up the past in Mrs Ackroid's bosom. But late on Saturday morning, Mrs Jenkins announced, 'If you think you're rid of that amnesiac, forget it. He's outside.'

I greeted him cheerfully in the consulting room. 'Everything coming back? The recorded highlights of your existence? Do you remember, do you remember, the house where you were born? The happiest days of your life at school? Your blissful wedding morn? But of course, you're not married.

He said nervously, 'That's the trouble, doctor, I think I am. As far as I can recollect, to a Mrs Cranshaw.'

'Well, well.'

'If I am one of your patients, doctor,' he continued uneasily, 'it follows that she'd be too, doesn't it? I wondered if you could oblige with my address.'

I buzzed Mrs Jenkins. After a couple of minutes she buzzed back. We had no Mrs Cranshaw.

'Possibly you left her somewhere around the North Sea,' I suggested to the patient.

He looked more uncomfortable. 'That's another worry, doctor. I do not apparently work in the North Sea.'

'Really? Mrs Ackroid thinks you do.'

He nodded. 'When she got home from the burgers last Monday evening, she said she was real concerned I wasn't at work, I'd got to make the effort, pull myself together, all that. On Tuesday morning she cuts me some meat-loaf sandwiches and helps me into my overcoat and kisses me goodbye on the doorstep. So I just follow people hurrying down the road and find myself at the station, where I took a train for London, as in the general direction of the North Sea. Then a red-faced bloke with a briefcase gets in the carriage and says breezily, "Hello! Anything wrong yesterday? We missed you after the weekend." I said quickly I'd been bilious. He said, "Yes, we thought something like that, if Mrs Edlington said you'd looked peaky once she said it a hundred times." '

'Who's Mrs Edlington?' I asked the patient.

'My mum, for all I knew. I was scared of a tricky conversation, but luckily he read the *Telegraph* until we arrived at Charing Cross terminus, where he said, "It's a fine frosty morning, let's walk to the office." It wasn't far, big white building on the river, the red-faced bloke talked all the time about projects, schedules, agendas, budgets, could have been talking about elephant-breeding for all I understood. There was a hall with rubber plants and a bloke in a blue uniform, we went up in the lift to a big room where I found a desk, and people kept coming up and asking if I was all right now and telling me to take care of myself.'

I asked keenly, 'But you *did* remember your work?'

'No, but it appeared I was in some government office, and this did not seem to matter. I just sat, and shuffled about some papers, and drank cups of tea, and everyone called me Mr Cranshaw and asked after Mrs Cranshaw.'

'What about the rest of the week?'

'I thought it best to go on being bilious.'

I suddenly realized this would make a splendid paper for the *BMJ*, if not the *British Journal of Psychiatry* or indeed *Brain*.

'Look, why not bring Mrs Ackroid along at the end of Monday evening surgery? We can discuss the entire problem in depth.'

He agreed readily. He seemed pitifully relieved at my continuing interest in his case. I assured him that meanwhile I should inquire if anyone local called Cranshaw had lost a husband.

Leaving after surgery for the golf club, I announced to Mrs Jenkins impressively, '*Unusual Complications of a Case of Amnesia in General Practice.* How's that as the title of the paper I'm writing for the *BMJ* on Mr Hemmings? Who as his case unfolds becomes a highly instructive patient, *not* a scrounging pseud.'

'I implore you, don't!' she cried. 'It's difficult enough already, explaining to new patients that you're an eccentric.'

'I am not in the slightest eccentric,' I said, offended.

'Oh, a perfectly competent eccentric, like Dr Samuel Johnson,' she assured me.

I told her stiffly, 'It will get my name in print and bring the practice considerable credit. Also, it will make the other Churchford GPs dead jealous. Particularly Dr Quaggy.'

Over the weekend I made a draft of my paper. I thought the case illustrated neatly Freud's conception of the libido as the high-tension electricity which drives us along our tracks of destiny, if sometimes off the rails. On Monday evening, Mr Hemmings and Mrs Ackroid appeared promptly, holding hands.

'I know all,' declared Mrs Ackroid soberly, as they sat in the consulting room. 'Charlie has told me about Mrs Cranshaw. It makes no difference. I shall always look upon Charlie as my own.'

I put my fingertips together. 'Mrs Cranshaw does not exist.'

'She exists at the office,' he objected.

'The office does not exist. My dear Mr Hemmings! Your case is perfectly straightforward. You just imagined going to this place. Mrs Cranshaw was just one of your hallucinations, like Norma.'

'Who's Norma?' demanded Mrs Ackroid.

I became aware of an unseemly commotion outside in the waiting room.

'Who's Norma?' Mrs Ackroid repeated more warmly.

An appalling thing happened. Mrs Jenkins threw open my door in the middle of a consultation.

'Mrs Cranshaw,' announced Mrs Jenkins, flushed. 'Demanding to see the doctor.'

I jumped up. 'This is perfectly outrageous.'

But Mrs Cranshaw was already in the consulting room, a pretty short-haired blonde with freckles. She pointed at Mr Hemmings a quivering finger. Indeed, she was quivering all over.

'I wants me husband back. One of my friends what comes for the water on her knees spotted him in the waiting room last Monday morning. What are you doing with my Eric, you bitch?' she demanded of Mrs Ackroid.

'Kindly leave the surgery,' I directed severely.

'You're in it too, I bet.' She rounded on me. 'Yes, you are, don't try denying it, I can see the guilt written over your face plainer than Heinz on a tin of beans. I'm going to report you to the National Health, I know my rights, I don't slave all day giving out tickets at parking meters for nothing, you come home, Eric.' She grabbed his sleeve.

'You stay right here with me, Charlie,' ordered Mrs Ackroid, grabbing the other.

'Mrs Jenkins,' I implored, as the two started shouting at each other. 'Restore decorum.'

'How?' she asked, flustered. 'With dogs they use a bucket of water.'

'Ladies, *please*!' I laid a calming hand on the struggling shoulders of both. 'Unseemly violence has no place in the domestic field, as it has not in the sporting one. Won't you allow me to blow the whistle and act impartially as referee? Mrs Ackroid, however devoted to Mr Cranshaw, is not married to him. Mrs Cranshaw is. So Mrs Cranshaw can keep him.'

Charlie-Eric grasped his forehead. 'Doctor! It's all coming back! I'm cured!'

'Excellent!' I congratulated him. 'At least some good's come out of this rough house.'

'I remember now! Clear as crystal. I'm not married to her.'

'Yes, you are,' objected Mrs Cranshaw.

'I only promised to marry her. Didn't I, love?'

'It's the same thing, as far as the neighbours are concerned,' said Mrs Cranshaw briskly.

'What about *my* neighbours?' demanded Mrs Ackroid threateningly. 'They were already calling me the Elizabeth Taylor of Rosemary Road when my husband walked out.'

From the open door, Mrs Wilberforce exclaimed, 'Herbert! What *are* you up to? Thank God I've found you. The children are asking awkward questions.'

'What's that woman doing here?' complained Mrs Cranshaw angrily.

'I came to see the doctor about my asthma. And what's my husband doing here, may I ask?'

'He's lost his memory,' I replied briefly. 'Just as I diagnosed.'

'And these are two nurses from some institution, I presume?'

'Don't you talk to me like that in front of my husband,' snapped Mrs Ackroid.

'Nor in front of mine,' added Mrs Cranshaw.

'This is going to complicate your paper for the *BMJ*,' murmured Mrs Jenkins. 'Might I suggest the title *A Case of Amnesia Amorosa*?'

'Bugger the *BMJ*,' I exclaimed. 'No one would believe it if I sent it to *The Guinness Book of Records*.' I demanded impatiently of Charlie-Eric-Herbert, 'Is *this* your lawful, as distinct from your other, wedded wives?'

'I don't know. I've gone blank again. Totally. Sorry.'

'You'd better ask British Airways.' Mrs Cranshaw suddenly sounded resigned. 'Eric works for them as a steward.' She began to cry.

'Charlie! Love! Surely you'd never forget *me*?' Mrs Ackroid began to cry.

'It's really very difficult,' he protested mildly. 'But you see, I've never set eyes on all three of you in my life.'

33

The ice of Mrs Wilberforce's schoolmistressy sang-froid melted. She began to cry.

'I've an urgent call from the St Boniface Twilight Home,' I announced.

I dashed through the door. 'Mrs Jenkins,' I panted in the waiting room. 'I apologize. That fellow is no more an invalid than Baron Münchausen was a pillar of truth. Call the police and have him arrested.'

'What for?' she asked, wide-eyed.

'Living off immoral earnings, I should imagine.'

'Honestly, doctor, I don't think the poor man's to blame. He just got into the hands of three selfish women, that's all.' Her eyes dropped. 'Last Saturday when we were alone in the waiting room, he chatted me up a bit. I don't think him a bad sort of feller at all.'

'*Et tu*, Jenkins!' I cried. I slammed the front door. A pretty redhead in jeans stood in my way.

'You the doctor?'

'Yes.'

'You got my Fred inside.'

'Feel free, go in, stake a claim,' I invited. 'And the very best of British luck.'

I jumped in the car. What to do? My professional duty was discharged. I shrugged. I drove off. It would clearly be best to let themselves sort it all out. It was snowing again. 'Thank God today's the end of bloody February,' I muttered.

But it was leap year. I had forgotten.

5

My young friend Dr Lonelyhearts makes a fortune from resolving such intimate perplexities as *Is It Normal to Hate My Mother?* Or, *Would Plastic Surgery Restore My Husband's Love?* Or, *Can I Get Pregnant if We Do It Standing Up?*

He is A Harley Street Specialist in the women's magazines. In the racier dailies he becomes A Doctor Speaks, on items like *Blackheads Can Be Beautiful* or *Understanding Your Piles*. In the serious papers he rises to Our Medical Correspondent, expounding authoritatively on such conditions of national importance as Benn's Legs, Michael's Foot, Thatcher's Eye, Steel's Blues and Princess Preggers.

The predicament of Britons infected by typhoid in Greece, bitten by mad dogs in Spain, sewn back to their arms and legs, struck by lightning, poisoned by hamburgers, frightened by spiders, he elucidates expertly overnight. He produces equally cheerful paperbacks on keeping fit and being ill. He whips up frothy articles on the latest fashionable diseases while his wife makes his dinner. I believe herpes and AIDS bought his Porsche. He relieves mail-order medicine with zesty, intelligent hospital thrillers like *Death in Coma*, *Lethal Angel* and *Needleprick*. Several other Dr Lonelyhearts share this raffish subculture of medicine, living more skittishly off printer's ink than patients' blood. The public consult them by post rather than their own GPs. A paper doctor, like a paper tiger, is less frightening.

Dr Lonelyhearts is Dr Aleyn Price-Browne BM from Oxford. He is tall, gingery and genial, in costly casual clothes like a rising actor relishing the respectability of success. His wife is pretty Dr Josephine from Guy's. Like many medical women with small children she works part-time in family planning, and doubtless finds it dispiriting always to play the waitress at the feast of love.

As the Lonelyhearts live nearby in Churchford, one sunny Sunday morning in March Sandra and I asked them home to the Old Surgery in Foxglove Lane for drinks. We were shortly into fascinating literary talk.

'Inside every bad novelist is a great novel struggling to get out, luckily unavailingly,' expanded Dr Lonelyhearts, who likes to control an unruly conversation by firing epigrams like rubber bullets,

'But you're going to write a *wonderful* novel one day, aren't you, darling?' encouraged Josephine. (Dr Lonelyhearts told me once that all authors' wives are married to Tolstoy.)

'It might win the Booker Prize,' suggested Sandra respectfully, offering nuts.

He laughed heartily. 'The British aren't in the slightest interested in authors, but they love a contest. Everything from the Boat Race to the Grand National, the bigger the field, the riskier the odds, the better the fun. The Booker on telly has raised contemporary English literature to the level of championship snooker. I raise my glass.'

Sandra looked disturbed, sharing Mrs Leo Hunter's esteem of authors.

'The public buy the lucky winner's book and feel literary,' he continued authoritatively. 'Just like they buy slimming books and feel slim. People seldom read what they buy. Or buy what they read. They get it free from the public library.'

'I must confess, I haven't bought many books,' said Sandra, subdued. 'Since *The Country Diary of an Edwardian Lady*.'

This made him muse, 'Why does any book catch on? Like the yo-yo, then the hula-hoop, now the home computer, everyone's got to have one. Good solid British snobbery, of course. There's royalties in royalty and the titles of the titled. Any publisher would give his eye teeth for the secret, if not his more cherished organs.'

Attending his glass with Glenmorangie, I ventured a protest. 'Surely the Booker Prize and suchlike are awarded by intellectuals to mark works of high literary value?'

'How do we know?' he asked. 'Until the author obliges by being dead for a hundred years. As my *Companion to English Literature* begins – with astringent Oxford scholarship – "Contemporary judgement is notoriously fickle and tends to be impassioned." ' He added amiably, 'For all publishers' airs, it's only the genteel end of showbiz.'

'We were in Norfolk last weekend with ours.' Josephine shivered. 'Thermal underwear time.'

'It is a truth universally acknowledged, as Jane Austen put it, that every London publisher has the ambition to become a country gentleman,' Dr Lonelyhearts explained. 'Spending from Friday to Monday poking his pigs instead of screwing his authors. Mine owns an Elizabethan mansion with wall-to-wall draughts, fires which send the heat up the chimney and the smoke into the room, and nothing to do indoors except drink and play scrabble for ruinous stakes. He'd cunningly asked one of those Manhattan publishers who need air-conditioning like premature babies need incubators – who held the rights of some big American novel by some big American master of banality. The guest broke on the Sunday morning. After a tramp with the dogs in the sleet, he was ready to sign absolutely anything for escape to the Connaught Hotel in Mayfair.'

Dr Lonelyhearts warmed the chilly memory with Glenmorangie. He sighed. 'I *could* write the great novel, did I not prefer the squalid comforts of life.'

'Doesn't the Arts Council give grants?' ventured Sandra.

'God knows why,' he told her. 'If a man's intelligent enough to write a book, he's intelligent enough to hold a job. I wrote *Needleprick* between bleeps as a houseman. Oh, I know what Shaw said, "A true artist will let his wife starve, his children go barefoot, his mother drudge for his living at seventy, sooner than work for anything but his art." But that only tells us what everyone knows, that Shaw was an insensitive egoist. I prefer Evelyn Waugh's advice – "Anyone could write a novel given six weeks, pen, paper, and no telephone or wife." '

'I am *not* another of your inconveniences,' said Josephine tartly.

'Got the prezzy?' He twisted towards her in the armchair beside the fire.

From a businesslike doctor's handbag she handed a small plastic bag. He displayed between fingertips a soft greenish cube. 'The greatest thing since sliced manna,' he explained proudly. He offered it to Sandra. 'Taste.'

She took a nervous nibble. He sat like an angler with a fish nosing the bait.

'Mint sauce,' she decided. 'Mixed with seaweed.'

'That's the wondrous herbal tang,' he corrected her, 'suggestive of dew-sparkling dawn pastures, the salutary breezes of spring, the eventide scent of a physic garden. Richard—' He offered me a bite.

'Some nutty health food?'

'Warmer! This is Sana. From the sano nut. It's the government's new cheese.'

I groaned. 'Not another Lymeswold, with politicians on television eating it as bravely as their own words?'

'Sana will down-market Lymeswold to mousetraps. It is more than a cheese.' Dr Lonelyhearts held the remains like a specimen extracted by a difficult operation. 'It is an international triumph. Remember the island of Chanca? Which the Americans and the Russians were desperate to liberate, whether the inhabitants liked it or not? Outcry in Parliament, because Chanca's in the Commonwealth and it shouldn't have been the American President who got angry, it should have been the Queen.'

I nodded.

'Not that anyone had heard of the place, except kids doing O-levels,' he continued. 'Chanca's economy depends entirely on the sano bean, as the economy of Tanzania depends on cashew nuts and of Ghana on chokkies. That's colonial independence for you! Swapping the rule of Governors for the whims of suburban hostesses.'

He shot a severe glance towards our nut bowl.

'We've bought the entire sano crop for the next fifty years as Commonwealth Aid,' he revealed.

'So the British must eat algae-flavoured sponge rubber to help the Americans irritate the Russians?' I demanded indignantly. 'Really, Aleyn! Scandalous!'

'Just run-of-the-mill diplomacy,' Dr Lonelyhearts disagreed airily. 'The sano bean is but the acorn of a massive political oak,' he added darkly. 'In a forest to immortalize our present government as gloriously as the New Forest William the Conqueror. The sano bean is healthy polyunsaturated fat all through, slice it where you will. Absolutely free of those deadly polysaturated fats which the British public gorges in soggy chips, bacon and eggs, buttered crumpets, cheeseburgers and treacle tart, only restrained by the resulting fatal coronary. Sana cheese came under the nose of Sir Arbuthnot Beakspeare, chief medical mandarin in Whitehall – '

'He lectured us local GPs,' I recalled. 'Very instructive, if I did rather feel that God had decided to bring down the tablets of stone from the mountain himself.'

'Who wafted it under the nose of the Minister of Health, who charitably decided to bestow on British voters Sana cooking fat, Sana mock-egg, Sana steaks, Sana bangers and for all I know Sana Mars Bars. Then the Prime Minister got a whiff and determined to revolutionize the British diet.'

'There's a campaign in the paper,' Sandra interrupted.

He nodded. 'Yes, I'm writing it. Though I rate the Prime Minister's chances of separating the British public from cholesterol like Woodrow Wilson's of separating the American public from alcohol. Come to the doctors' preview on Tuesday, Richard. Big party in Park Lane.' As I looked doubtful, he added, 'You won't have to *eat* the revolting stuff, it's all free-loading champagne and lobster pâtés. I'm running the promotion.'

Leaving, Dr Lonelyhearts lowered his voice. 'Got any Panacea Drug shares?' I said no, after deliberation to give an impression of assets outside the building society. 'Lucky you! Their new wonder drug has been found to rot the kidneys. I heard last week at a conference in Miami. The shares will fall like the temperature of a corpse.'

'Isn't it appalling that people make money from human disasters?' I chided. 'Fleming spurned a penny from penicillin.'

'Only because the fool hadn't the nous to patent it. Just run-of-the-mill business,' he ended, zipping up his Barbour. 'Want a couple of stalls for Covent Garden? A drug company sent them, but I've a dinner at Claridge's.'

I acquainted Sandra with my acceptance of Dr Lonelyhearts' invitation.

'Don't let him lead you astray,' she said.

'Good God!' I exclaimed. 'That's like telling the Devil not to sell his soul to Faust.'

'You're only a humdrum GP of totally unsophisticated tastes,' she informed me. 'He's intimate with television people and politicians, and you've only got to read the papers.'

I poured myself another Glenmorangie.

'Though come to think of it,' I mused, 'what would anyone give for a battered, grimy old soul like mine?'

6

I attended the Park Lane party from curiosity, not debauchery. I was fascinated by the heady, chancy, expense-account career of young Dr Lonelyhearts, playing his hand of credit cards, flaunting his mastery of airline timetables, enjoying through the (equally tax-deductible) liberality of drug companies the life of itinerant extravagance once led by the sons of dukes dispatched upon the Grand Tour.

The hotel ballroom was already full of middle-aged, dowdyish men and women chattering light-heartedly and drinking purposefully, the medical profession with its bleep switched off. I recognized lean, tall Sir Arbuthnot Beakspeare conversing with Sir Rollo Basingstoke, my contemporary at St Swithin's, who disguised his shock at seeing me in such powerful professional company with the suavity befitting a Surgeon to the Queen.

On a dais with lights and microphones, Dr Lonelyhearts talked forcefully to a scruffy, restless group, the press. Cheerful, elegant black gentlemen sat round a table with the pink Chancan flag, enjoying a windfall from the British taxpayer more lavish than bestowed by their Caribbean hurricanes. I sipped Bollinger until Dr Lonelyhearts began through a microphone, 'My Lords, ladies and gentlemen.

'This occasion, I venture to say,' he continued solemnly, 'will compare in history to that day in 1587 when Sir Walter Raleigh brought from the fields of Virginia to our shores the homely, invaluable, beloved potato.'

Nobody laughed. It was his champagne.

Dr Lonelyhearts humbly preferred not wasting the time of his distinguished audience with a sadly inexpert dissertation on the wondrous new food shortly to satisfy our appetites and tickle our palates, while conferring a benefit upon the health of the nation, he ventured to say, comparable with that performed upon the health of the Royal Navy by the brilliant Edinburgh physician James Lind in 1753, with his miraculous introduction of lemon juice to cure scurvy at sea.

Dr Lonelyhearts paused impressively.

'I should prefer leaving that to another Scotsman of genius, Andrew McGoggin, Professor of Nutrition at Scone University. Sana,' he ended with hushed reverence, 'is his brainchild.'

To applause led enthusiastically by Dr Lonelyhearts, there arose a slight man resembling a skull wearing skin a size too small. It appeared through an accent as thick as a Highlander's plaid that the professor passed his leisure shinning up and down the Cairngorms on a grated carrot, a pinch of oatmeal, a bite of honeycomb. He hated food as Daniel hated lions, the Ancient Mariner the albatross, Prometheus eagles. Eating was a pleasure as idiotic as playing Russian roulette, the arts of cookery as repulsive as the temptations of Jezebel, food writers viler than pornographers, restaurants gastric brothels. We should be rigorously educated to regard food only as the body's diesel oil.

Suddenly the room was full of pretty girls in white with piled trays of Sana cheese. Sir Arbuthnot gobbled his ration like a seal leaping for sprats. Sir Rollo stealthily dropped his among the daffodils. I found Dr Lonelyhearts beside me.

'Sorry I didn't have the chance for a chat,' he said breathlessly. 'Wasn't much fun, was it? Come to the big Guildhall national launch in a fortnight, it'll make this look like a school dinner. Yes, you must,' he insisted. 'The Minister's appearing himself. That dreadful hookworm Quaggy was wriggling after an invitation only yesterday.'

'Did he mention me?' I remarked curiously. 'That they were already stocking up with single malts for my booking at the St Boniface Twilight Home?'

'Oh, he was quite flattering. Said you were Churchford's answer to Mr Pickwick. Particularly since you'd been putting on weight.'

The following week Sana hit the British public – like everything else, from royal marriages to the Cup Final, through their TV screens.

Clean-cut athletes ran like Derby winners, high-jumped weightlessly, swam like torpedoes, then reached for a slice of Sana cheese as goggle-eyed as Billy Bunter reaching into his tuckbox. These commercials conflicted with others depicting slim, sexy girls munching slices of everyday cheeses, eyes half-closed, like the whores of Babylon reaching for aphrodisiacs. I found this confusing.

Equally perplexing that week was the epidemic of March fever. My patients exhibiting a temperature, vomiting and diarrhoea all claimed they had it. I had never heard of March fever. But doctor! they protested unbelievingly, it's in all the papers.

That weekend I was called as GP to the Lonelyhearts' six-year-old son, who had bellyache. Like all medical parents they suspected appendicitis, peritonitis, or nasty abdominal conditions never seen outside examination papers. After reassuring Dr Lonelyhearts, I inquired over a Laphroaig about the clash of television advertising.

He replied off-handedly, 'You can't expect the butter-and-egg trade to give up without a fight.'

'You mean, the traditional cheesemongers have joined forces to repel invaders of their market?'

'Surely you remember the butter boys' gruesome adverts depicting margarine as vitaminized axle grease? And the margarine people twisting medical statistics to portray a slice of bread and butter as the mat on a well-polished helter-skelter to the grave?'

I protested, 'But what about this healthy revolution in the British diet, so dear to our Prime Minister's heart?'

'Oh, marketing isn't interested in health, which has no cash value. Otherwise the big tobacco and booze companies would go into voluntary liquidation tomorrow, wouldn't they?'

'Profits from pathology and dividends from disease strike me as immoral,' I said forthrightly.

'Only run-of-the-mill big business,' he responded easily. 'So young George upstairs is going to live?'

'He's suffering from nothing worse than March fever,' I informed him. 'There's a lot of it about.'

To my consternation, Dr Lonelyhearts roared with laughter. I inquired the joke.

'I invented it,' he explained cheerfully. 'There's some sort of gastric flu going round, and my editor wanted a snappy name so the sufferers could say they'd read about it in his paper.'

'I think that's unethical,' I remonstrated sternly.

'Just run-of-the-mill journalism. Don't forget the Guildhall on Wednesday. By the way, I'm on the other side now. Organizing the promotion with those lovely girls eating fatty old Stilton and Camembert and Double Gloucester. More money. Run-of-the-mill PR,' he ended airily.

Dr Lonelyhearts' coterie seemed to embrace the loyalties exhibited by the Roman senate in the last days of Julius Caesar.

I arrived promptly at the Guildhall, embedded in the City of London. I discovered Dr Lonelyhearts emerging, pale and trembling. I solicitously suggested an attack of March fever. Shaking his head impatiently, he leaned against the civic stonework and exclaimed chokingly, 'Curried nut roast.'

'Nut what?'

'Your lunch,' he explained. 'Also spinach pasties, cucumber and yoghurt salad, rice-stuffed cabbage leaves and toasted sunflower seeds. My gastric mucosa,' he continued angrily, 'had its napkin tucked under its chin awaiting turtle soup followed by roast sirloin and Yorkshire pud. My successor,' he spluttered, 'has succumbed to the perverted notions of that raving Scots fakir and provided this totally inedible wholefood.'

I stood aghast.

'Worse—' Dr Lonelyhearts steadied himself. He added in the voice of Mr Bumble to Oliver Twist, '*No booze!*'

Medicine teaches you to think on your feet. 'Let's find a pub and get prophylactically pissed.'

Too late! A black Rover, green-uniformed lady at the wheel, emitted the Minister of Health. He was short, pasty, fat, and puffed inside gripping the arm of his fellow-passenger, lofty Sir Arbuthnot.

'He doesn't look very well,' I exclaimed.

Dr Lonelyhearts agreed. 'But today's launch is so essential for his ambitious career, I doubt if he'd have been put off coming even by death.'

'Surely,' I objected, 'he's our famous caring politician, always keeping open threatened little inefficient hospitals, firing the starting pistol for wheelchair marathons, and seeing sick kids are submitted to appallingly dangerous heart operations?'

'I believe every night he thanks God for making his fellow-beings ill, disabled and poor. They're his parliamentary bread and butter, like other MPs who specialize in rape, paedophilia, hare coursing or the Royal Navy, but easier. In opposition, you accuse the government of cruelty for corking the cornucopias of the NHS. In government, you take credit for everything, including startled women on fertility drugs with septuplets.' I looked unbelieving. He grinned. 'Politics is the art of the cynical.'

The anteroom was full of important-looking people staring into glasses of orange juice with the gloom of those committed to a lunch for rabbits. Dr Lonelyhearts introduced Sir Arbuthnot.

'You GPs really should instruct your patients in healthy, nutritious diets,' he said with the fearsome condescension of a hearty headmaster. 'Do far more good than all those tranquillizers you insist on prescribing at the government's expense. Perfectly easy, only take you half an hour.'

I explained, 'If I gave half-hours to all my patients I should be conducting a twenty-four-hour surgery and the waiting room would never get cleaned.'

But he did not seem to hear. 'This significant occasion is unfortunately marred by our splendid Minister suffering a little tummy trouble,' he lamented. 'Fortunately, I have this in hand. I examined him at the Ministry and diagnosed March fever.'

'Very shrewd,' murmured Dr Lonelyhearts.

'Yes, sometimes the condition presents difficulties in recognition.'

Lunch was announced, to faint enthusiasm. A bishop intoned grace, incorporating a nasty crack about the value of fasting. We filled long tables splendid with silver and flowers, munching sullenly until the Queen's health was drunk in sparkling Malvern water and the toastmaster announced, 'You may not smoke.'

Over the decaffeinated coffee with skimmed milk and saccharine arose the Minister.

Instantly there were lights, television cameras clicking as noisily as roosting starlings, a phallic forest of microphones.

'This magnificent British product,' the Minister began, 'the peerless British cheese, shortly to spread nutrition and delight in British homes...'

He stopped. He ground his teeth. He took a sip of water. He continued as though overcome with the emotion of his message. I noticed him clutch the lower waistcoat. I frowned. Acute appendicitis? But what was the diagnosis of a humble GP, against a doctor who could direct the health of the nation without taking his elbows from his blotter?

The peroration implied that Sana cheese was the healthiest substance discovered since fresh air. A gold-frogged man in scarlet stood with a silver salver of it. The Minister raised a chunk to the TV cameras and ate it.

'Delicious,' he murmured ecstatically.

Then he belched, gurgled, vomited into the freesias and sank groaning to the floor.

Pandemonium.

The bishop nervously inquired if he needed the final blessing, or his brow wiped with a damp napkin? Sir Arbuthnot leaped to his patient complaining this was the first fulminating case of March fever and he would immediately phone the *Lancet*. Scarlet-coated flunkies bore the moaning Minister to some distant mayoral sofa. Ashen-faced men in striped trousers consulted whisperingly. Police inspectors barked into squawking walkie-talkies for ambulances. The soberly vengeful press recorded each writhe and grimace, before dashing to Fleet Street with the best launching story since Henry VIII's *Mary Rose*.

Dr Lonelyhearts sat quietly beside me.

'The Minister's freed us for a Glenfiddich before closing time,' he observed. 'I suspect his only uncalculated kindness for years.'

The perforated appendix was removed at nearby Bart's. The Minister recovered, but not his career. He was shortly shuffled to Transport. The only use Sana achieved was a feed for comics on TV.

I next encountered Dr Lonelyhearts on a pouring afternoon leaving the Perfect Gent, our smart outfitters near Robbins Modes in Churchford High Street.

'Kitting myself with tropical gear for Chanca,' he greeted me heartily. 'Where the cheese comes from.'

'The political situation seems defused out there,' I said, staring enviously under my umbrella.

'Indeed. But the British government has in addition to egg on its face thousands of tons of Sana cheese on its hands. So we're shipping it out to Chanca, as Commonwealth Aid. I believe there's enough to feed the population with every meal for a generation. That'll teach the buggers to flirt with the Russians. I've landed the contract for the promotion,' he disclosed proudly. 'Which shouldn't be difficult, as they can't send the muck back. So at last I've got that six weeks in the sun without telephone or wife, to write one of the world's great novels. Pity I'll miss the Cup Final. Care for a couple of seats? I was sent them by a drug company. Who knows, it may stop raining?'

I thanked him. People like Dr Lonelyhearts always win. They pick opponents who continue to score own goals.

7

'April is the cruellest month,' I informed Sandra over breakfast on the 1st.

'It isn't, it's the Oh, to be in England month.'

'There's ample differential diagnosis in poetry. Death can be easeful or a fell sergeant. Woman can be the name of frailty or uncertain, coy and hard to please. Love conquers all, or is a malady without a cure.'

'Why was Eliot so beastly to April?'

'Because it mixes memory and desire. Perhaps he just meant the brighter days make people reflect it's a long time since they had it? It's been proved to work with pigeons.' I mused, thinking of patients' family upsets, 'He's right, the spring rain stirs our dull roots.'

'Yes, I'm thinking of taking a job,' she announced.

'Oh?'

'After all, I don't want to be another of those bored suburban housewives.'

'No, of course not,' I concurred readily. 'But don't the Friends of the General provide a pleasant occupation?'

'Not since they've all fallen out.'

'What employment had you in mind?'

'Nursing, naturally. It's sheer laziness for a woman to let maternity wreck her career or her figure.'

'The St Boniface Twilight Home would welcome another oar in the lifeboat,' I suggested encouragingly. 'Yes, it's ridiculous that rearing children should blow a hole in a useful job. Which is going to be Jilly's problem. The NHS has estimably unsexist views on maternity leave, but equality will hit the surgical profession only when the rising young men are forced to take nine months' holiday two or three years in succession.'

'But there's no satisfaction like the primeval one of bringing up a family.'

I agreed. 'Though I can't actually remember doing anything to bring up Andy and Jilly. I was so busy getting the practice going, I don't fancy I took much notice of either until they were old enough to stand me half a pint in a pub. Child-rearing is anyway largely the instilling of parental prejudices. Luckily, whatever you do, they shoot up like asparagus.'

I promised her to tout for work.

My first patient that pleasant spring morning was Gwen Watson, in the stylish Oxford-blue uniform of St Ursula's. Churchford's independent girls' school flourishes academically and financially under the forthright headmistresship of Mrs Rosalie Charrington, who each speech day distributes with irrepressible pride the glittering prizes to an age still uninstructed how easily these become tarnished.

St Ursula's credit belongs more fairly to the genes of thrusting entrepreneurs from the mean and leafless city streets, settled amid the patios and barbecues of our desirable residences. No leap up the gnarled branches of British society exacts more ability and ambition than lower-middle to middle-middle class. Clogs may revert to clogs in three generations, but Gwen's generation was well-heeled in sharp-witted spikes.

'I've got my bike,' she responded breathlessly to my concern at her missing assembly. She dropped her crammed satchel on the consulting-room floor. 'And Miss Brownlow, who's in charge of religious knowledge and the Yamaha, is always late.'

'How's Mum and Dad?'

'All right.'

Sandra and I regularly took Sunday morning drinks in their Neo-Georgian home, where the windows were darkened by vast shiny green plants and the garden floodlit at night. The Watsons were young, active, unimaginatively comfortable, conventionally hedonistic, fastidiously genteel, unaffectedly tasteless and innocently smug. They were like everyone's neighbours in Churchford.

49

I glanced at Gwen's card. Time's winged chariot was supersonic. 'Fifteen last birthday?'

'That's right.'

'Well, young lady. What can I do for you?'

'I want to go on the pill.'

'Ah.'

We assessed each other.

As Caliban with Miranda, I realized suddenly she was no longer a child. I viewed her with some boyfriend's eye of love. She had brown hair, bright cheeks, lovely legs in black tights, green eyes as soft as peeled grapes, lips as inviting as first strawberries, and tits like ripening melons (Charentais). She was as sexually mature as any mother of five. Once a girl's endocrine glands take off at puberty, they woosh like an airliner's jets until landing on the sunset-flowing tarmac of the menopause, barring equally unfortunate accidents.

'It's perfectly legal, isn't it?' She was steeling herself for heart-wrenching disappointment. 'My friend Sally Siddons at school, she's terribly sophisticated, her dad's in television, told me there wasn't a law against it.'

'Well, yes,' I said. 'Well, no,' I said.

She laughed nervously. 'It's silly, but I haven't even *seen* the pill, I mean, is it like the saccharins Mrs Charrington puts in her coffee at break, or the things Libby Parrish showed us that she gives her horses?'

'Do your parents know about this?'

She gasped. 'Oh, no! My mother would kill me.'

She had open-ended apprehension that I might deliver pills like a bubblegum machine or as easily grass to Mrs Charrington, lecture her like Mr Podsnap (more truthfully Mr Pecksniff), pray for her soul or box her ears. My urge was to bang the desk, tear my wisps of hair and shout, 'You stupid little twit! Why do you want to raise appalling medico-socio-legal problems? Can't you wait till after breakfast on your sixteenth birthday?'

Instead, I said, 'The Queen in Parliament has every right to keep you off sex, but you have every right to keep me to my Hippocratic Oath. All this remains our big secret. Do you want the pill *today*?' A remarkable aspect of sexual activity is the immediate urgency with which it is approached. 'Or is it blanket cover, if I may so put it?'

'I'd never do it with anyone but Edgar,' she replied solemnly. 'He's really lovely, like Jimmy Connors but heaps younger. I met him playing hockey in the Christmas hols.'

'How do you rate your chances with A-levels?'

She was startled at such prosaic irrelevance. 'Mrs Charrington says three A-grades, if I apply myself diligently. Which would be brill.'

'Right. You're an intelligent young woman. We can discuss your predicament with the sense it seldom attracts. Middle-aged ladies sing in their delightful hot bubble baths of indignation about wicked doctors overriding the sacred rights of parents. Judges shudder in their wigs at reckless medical men handing girls a season ticket to promiscuity – which is far worse, because it outrages the law. But sex regrettably happens whether Mummy likes it or not. Otherwise, there would be no teenage pregnancies to prevent, would there?'

She nodded. I continued the lecture, 'Of all contraceptives, pregnophobia – understand? – is easily the least effective. Pregnancy is not in the forefront of the mind at the time. If you're using contraceptives or toothpaste, you might as well use the most efficient one. Right? Hence the pill. The most telling argument against is randy teenagers forgetting to take it.'

'I'd remember,' she assured me. 'Mummy always taught me to take a spoonful of Petrolagar regularly on Saturday night.'

'Unlike lawyers, who – as a hockey player, you'll appreciate – love the rules more than the game, we doctors have to work in a real world. And deceitful daughters, my dear Gwen, are as bothersome in it as shocked mothers.'

She looked abashed. I said, 'Let's soften the hard corners of family life. I advise you to risk the parental frown of disapproval and tell Mum.'

'Yes, I'm sure I should, really,' she agreed. 'But, well, I don't know, Mummy seems more terrified at me having sex than the dog getting run over.'

'And Daddy?'

51

She giggled. 'He seems to think my virginity is somehow a reflection on himself, like his golf handicap.'

'Take heart, two out of three girls who slip into the doctor's like you tell Mum in the end, even in families as quarrelsome as the United Nations. You'd better be peddling along. Miss Brownlow will be warming up on the Yamaha.'

Ah, the pill! I reflected. Like the television set, a vehicle of mass entertainment and few people know how it works. Simple, reliable, invisible, cheap – and toxic – the pill is a manufactured mixture of hormones naturally secreted by the ovary. They suppress the expulsion of the egg, a sensitive and regulated mechanism in all mammals. They operate by negative feedback on the body's power pack, round the tiny pituitary gland at the base of the brain.

The morning-after pill, like the intrauterine coil, works by preventing implantation of the fertilized egg in the wall of the womb. Minds shuttered with prejudice, or dimmed by the light of stained glass, accuse it of abortion, not contraception. But it was cleared by our lawyers, whose amazing knowledge of the interior of the human uterus I sometimes feel rivals the sperm's.

The following morning, I was myself struck with open-ended apprehension. Bill Watson strode into the consulting room.

Gwen's father was big, handsome, fair, wearing a tailored suit with a bright tie and matching handkerchief frothing from his pocket, a monogrammed shirt and a watch which could unexpectedly burst into bleeps. He made a fortune from saunas, solarias and jacuzzis. His combined model had the public paying eagerly for the sensation of sitting up to its neck in a swirling river at noon in the steamy tropics.

'How's the golf, Richard?' he started, always betokening embarrassment.

'Fine. How's the family?'

'We have our little problems.' He fixed me with an aggressive eye. 'I've come on a bit of delicate business.'

Had Gwen followed my advice? Was her father concealing a horsewhip? Or an automatic? Churchford had rumours of his own father being a timorously respected Hackney gangster.

I struck pre-emptively. 'The pill?'

He gasped. 'Honest! You doctors! Actual clairvoyants. I wish I'd half the gift with my customers.'

'Well, it can't be for you,' I pointed out.

'But it is!' He gave a laugh, then looked solemn. 'Mrs Lamboni, my secretary, is a woman in a million.'

'Ah.'

'There's a very sensitive bond between us.' He became even graver. 'We vibrate together, quite amazingly.' He looked funereal.

'Good,' I remarked.

'So you see, Richard, I'd like a prescription for the pill. Though not a word all round,' he added hastily. 'Otherwise Mr Lamboni, not to mention Mrs Watson, might feel emotionally disturbed.'

I asked stiffly, 'Mrs Lamboni, I presume, has her own doctor?'

'I suppose so, down Balham way, where she lives.'

'I must enlighten you, Bill, about the Hippocratic Oath. Prescribing for other doctors' patients is a worse sin than poking other men's wives.'

He looked nervous. 'But if Mrs Lamboni went to her own GP, maybe her husband would find out. He'd kill her. And I do not use figures of speech. He's a Sicilian. In the cooked-meat trade, Italian sausage and that.'

'I don't want to be an accessory to a crime passionnel, but you must take my point.'

He nodded dejectedly. 'No pill?'

'Not from me. How's young Gwen?' I inquired.

His face lit as instantly as a striking match.

'Wonderful! Nothing but hockey, out practising dribbling on the patio before breakfast. Mad on it! Isn't it lovely, the age of innocence before tormenting sex problems? Come to think of it,' he added sombrely, rising and shaking hands, 'I believe that Mr Lamboni would probably kill me, too.'

Settled in our Victorian villa in Foxglove Lane with a glass of Macallan at my elbow after my day's work, I reached for the ringing telephone.

'Richard? Pam Watson here.'

Open-ended apprehension. Did she suspect Bill's keen interest in Mrs Lamboni's reproductive cycle? That Gwen's hockey fetish romped on a sexual field? Would she too apply a blowlamp to assay the precious metal of my Hippocratic Oath? But she was only asking us to Sunday drinks.

As Sandra was visiting Mother, I suggested enlivening Jilly's day off from the General. Lovely! They'd asked Mrs Henderson, who would adore to tell Jilly about her terribly interesting gallbladder.

Jilly drove me in her Metro. The Watsons had a Rolls, Volvo and Suzuki, televisions and videos, microwaves and computers, players and recorders, the compact electronics with which the successful inhabitants of Churchford embellish their homes, as those of Amazonia once with the shrunken heads of their enemies.

'I've gone back to work,' Pam Watson imparted at once. She was pretty like Gwen, except the melons were Honeydew.

'I've started with Pangloss Enterprises in Mayfair,' she continued eagerly. 'You know, they do absolutely everything. I'm reception hostess.'

I congratulated her, sipping my Glenlivet by the double-glazing overlooking the lily pond and garden statuary.

'Did you know I was Bill's secretary when he started in business?' She simpered. 'He used to say I was a woman in a million. Yes, it's quite a challenge. But now Gwen's young brothers are both at boarding school, I mustn't be just another bored suburban housewife, must I?'

I nodded towards Gwen, prim in white blouse and check skirt, distributing the Twiglets. 'She's ever so happy these days,' said Pam, 'now she's getting it regularly.'

'Pardon?'

'Hockey,' she explained. 'Keeps her wonderfully fit, she wouldn't even *look* at a drink, not like some of those dreadful teenagers in the lovely homes round here, you wouldn't believe. Gwen would never overdo it because she knows that Mummy wouldn't like it, but it's terrifying the influences going against parents' wishes in our hard-nosed society.'

I had a word with Gwen under the pretence of requiring Twiglets. 'You've said nothing?' I murmured.

'No, but I'm going to soon,' she whispered. 'It's not something you can just bring up, like saying you want to go on a diet. Can I fetch you another drink? Daddy expected you'd finish the bottle, but there's lots to go.'

I discussed the Watson ethics trap with Jilly driving home. As she was my colleague as well as my daughter, the Oath was switched off.

Jilly asked, 'Who do you think would outrage Pam Watson more, secretly seeking the pill? Her husband or her daughter?'

'Her daughter,' I answered readily. 'Some parents demand from their children an obedience and devotion which they know would be utterly impossible to demand from their spouses.'

'Who are big enough to walk out.'

'It's parental insecurity,' I decided. 'Perhaps they realize they're not really worthy of such burning love? You know, it always amazes me how few parents try to make friends of their children.'

'Or sometimes of their spouses,' sighed Jilly.

I continued warmly, 'Those excitable, indeed hysterical, self-assured, self-satisfied moralizing pressure groups give us doctors the blame for inciting the young to have sex all over the shop, never the credit for keeping an unfortunate third party out of these conflicts – the unborn baby.'

'Oh, it's doctors' own fault. Pretending we're more than mere cutters and purgers.' Jilly has the surgical mentality.

I repeated what the family had heard often enough. 'Medicine became mixed with morals once the public transferred its faith from the man in the surplice to the man in the white coat.'

We were passing St Alphege's parish church, Kentish ragstone amid yew-shaded acres embedded with tombstones, to emphasize the value of virtue when the prospect of Heaven was as real as that of next summer's holidays.

I observed sombrely, 'Which would never have happened had Freud been a rabbi, Darwin a bishop and Bertrand Russell a doctor.'

'Come off it, Daddy,' said Jilly.

8

Sandra had found her St Swithin's uniform in a trunk at her mother's. On Monday morning she donned it in our bedroom. A flattering fit. Her white dress, blue belt and black stockings mixed memory with desire.

'I heard there's a part-time job going at The Downs Private Clinic,' I told her. 'Good money.'

'I don't think I'll bother,' she said vaguely, twirling. 'If you're shortly going to retire.'

'You know I'm *not* going to retire,' I objected crossly. 'Lord Lister was looking after Queen Victoria years older than me.'

'It's just what I hear all over Churchford.' She was admiring herself in the mirror.

'Bloody Quaggy,' I muttered.

I left for the surgery. More open-handed apprehension. Pam Watson arrived, with her shopping.

'Richard—' She leaned forward earnestly in her chair. 'It's about our daughter. Something came out after the party.'

So Gwen had spoken up. That Sunday afternoon, both her parents with a hangover, too. Did Pam regard me as the gravest menace to teenage children since Fagin?

'Gwen discussed her embarrassing problem, did she?'

Pam stared admiringly. 'You doctors! Real mind readers. But of course! You were clever and noticed the first signs.'

'God! She's pregnant.'

'I should hope *not*!'

'Sorry.'

'It's her allergy.'

'To what?'

'Absolutely everything,' Pam said forthrightly. '*You* know. This total allergy syndrome. It's always getting in the newspapers. At least, I *suppose* that's what Gwen was going on about,' she continued uncertainly. 'You know how coy young girls are about their bodies? So I said, Gwen, darling, it's total allergy, but don't *worry*, Mummy will *look after you*, as Mummy always does, Mummy will go to the doctor about it first thing tomorrow morning.'

'Why couldn't she come to the doctor about it herself?' I demanded briskly.

'But she has to go to school.'

'She's got a bike. She could slip in before assembly and Miss Brownlow on the Yamaha.'

'I suppose so,' said Pam vaguely. 'Is there a pill or something you can give her?'

'I cannot prescribe without examining the patient. Hippocratic Oath.'

'Oh, well, perhaps Gwen will be all right if nature takes its course. She didn't seem desperately ill with it, I must say.' Pam fidgeted. 'Anyway, I wanted to consult you this morning, because there's something else.'

'About Gwen?'

'No. About me.' She crossed her legs. 'Richard –' She crossed them again.

'Yes?'

'You know I'm not on the pill? It's Bill, remember? He was terribly scared about it clotting the blood, you keep seeing it in the papers. Awfully sweet and considerate of him, really.'

She took a deep breath. 'Now I've this lovely new job in Mayfair, naturally there's a lot of social duties involved, you wouldn't believe the cocktail parties, I mean, absolutely no expense spared, but of course all to create business, Japanese and that, and honestly, some of the sales personnel are really quite nice, you know, *our* sort of class, and it would be more convenient if I was on the pill, but if Bill found out he would kill me.'

She looked at me nervously, like Gwen.

'Fine!' I rubbed my hands. 'Splendid. No problem. Your husband will never know. My Hippocratic Oath. Just one thing—'

'Yes?' she asked anxiously.

'Are you over sixteen?'

She exploded into hearty laughter, in which I joined.

I saw her to the surgery front door. Returning, I muttered, 'I know about family planning, but this is ridiculous.'

Mrs Jenkins was confused.

I imagined the Watsons gathered each evening at the television set brooding during the commercial breaks on their unspeakable secrets, their hearts blacker with guilt against the radiant innocence of the others'. How a prescription for the pill could flutter as emotively as Desdemona's handkerchief! Was I handling the case correctly? It might be unethical, but altogether kindlier, and possibly preclude them suffocating each other with their pillows, if I invited Bill, Pam and Gwen next Sunday for drinks, disclosed all and passed it off as a huge joke.

I decided even Hippocrates could not get away with this. Nor Oscar Wilde. Nor the three Marx Brothers.

On the Friday evening Bill Watson appeared at the surgery, too agitated even to start about golf.

'There's been a hiccup with Maria. That's Mrs Lamboni.' He fiddled with the gold buckle of his personalized leather belt. 'Maria's a sincere person. She was educated at a convent.'

I nodded approval.

'She's a thinking person, too,' he disclosed. 'She won't take as gospel what anyone tells her, not even the Pope. She's religious, mass and that, goes quite often I believe, but she doesn't think it's any more wicked to swallow the pill than haddock on Friday.'

'But her doctor in Balham's a Catholic, too'

'Clairvoyance again,' murmured Bill admiringly. 'He doesn't take such an easygoing view of sin and so on. Called her a loose woman. Much worse, in fact. I'd like a word or two with him, but I suppose I must respect his holy feelings. He utterly refused to give Mrs Lamboni the pill without Mr Lamboni's say-so. Mrs Lamboni refuses to take risks with me without it. OK. So what do I do?'

'How irksome that religion should become mixed with reproduction,' I mused. 'Quite as vexing as politics with sport. It gives the authorities of our present existence, and of our one hereafter, the chance to emphasize their importance through two activities which so valuably divert human minds from either.'

He did not seem to heed. 'Do you suppose this Balham doctor will let on?'

'It depends if he applies his Hippocratic Oath to the case as seriously as I have.'

'If even a hint got back to Mr Lamboni, it could be very embarrassing. Mr Lamboni is not one of your operatic Italians. No. He is a big fellow, with a big black moustache. I've seen him in the back of his shop in his white suit, slicing up a Parma ham like riffling the leaves of a book. I do not care for salami,' Bill remarked feelingly, 'and I do not wish to become one.'

'Try seeing his point of view,' I suggested reasonably. 'If fathers refuse daughters the pill to discourage promiscuity, the argument gathers force when applied to their wives, who also have free use of the car.'

Gwen carried the added handicap of sex not being allowed for in the scheme of any schoolchild's life. But she had a bicycle.

Bill looked shifty. 'There's something in that, I suppose. I'd never have Pam on the pill. For the same reason as the hot-blooded Mr Lamboni, doubtless. Can't you suggest anything?'

'Take a rather extensive shave one morning and slip out for a slick vasectomy.'

He was not enthusiastic. Men like Bill Watson imbue their vas deferens with the sanctity of Samson's hair.

That Saturday afternoon I drove to our popular Greenfinger Garden Centre, for compost-maker to mulch the autumn leaves. As I wandered among the delightful shelves of trowels, twine, secateurs, pest-killers, bird-scarers and dog-constipators, I encountered Pam Watson gazing soulfully at the Gro-bags.

After a cheerful interchange about chrysanthemums, I dropped my voice and asked discreetly, 'I hope the prescription is a success?'

She compressed her lips. 'I've torn it up,' she informed me. 'Yes! Torn it up. You wouldn't believe what swine some of those executives can be. If they spent their evenings watching video nasties, I shouldn't be in the slightest surprised.' She shuddered. 'Things certainly have changed since the days when Bill and I were courting, believe you me, I mean, permissiveness, well, I'm as broadminded as anyone, but perversion, really, no thank *you*. It's a great mistake to expose respectable married women to such employment.'

I commiserated with her return to bored suburban housewife.

'Not a bit,' she disclosed. 'Fortunately, I've effected a transfer to a better job. Personal assistant to the chairman, who is pushing seventy.'

Had I seen the last of the Watsons? If Gwen burst out her confession, they would both be too bored with the pill to take any notice. On Monday morning, I was startled to find my first patients all three of them. Gwen was in school uniform with her crammed satchel. They sat and stared at me big-eyed.

'Richard,' began Bill solemnly. 'All weekend we've been having an ongoing discussion in depth about ourselves.'

Open-ended apprehension! They had been lifting the skirts of their souls. Who now knew what I had said to whom? Who resented what I had not said to them about which? I kept safely silent.

'As you're our old friend, as well as our GP – ' Bill fidgeted with his gold identity bracelet. 'We'd like you to know that our marriage is going through a tricky phase.'

'Just getting bored with each other, I suppose.' Pam was staring into the far corner.

Bill nodded vigorously. 'Yes, that's the problem. Looking round our lovely home in Churchford I feel that God has been good to me, though mind you, I reckon I met him halfway. But even a Rolls doesn't make you happy, does it?'

'The only happy drivers seem teenagers on rowdy motorbikes.'

'Frankly, the fuse had burned right down under us,' he confessed. 'But we decided to make a fresh start, to stick together.' He added proudly, 'Because of young Gwen here.'

'She has a brilliant future,' declared Pam earnestly. 'Mrs Charrington told us.'

'Wonderful A-levels coming up,' agreed Bill. 'I'm learning. I always thought Garibaldi was a biscuit and Bunyan something you got on your foot.'

'I decided it was the insecurity giving her total allergy symptoms.' Pam squeezed her daughter. 'Didn't Mummy, darling?'

'Now that everybody's going to live happily ever after,' I said briskly, 'I'd like a word with Gwen about this allergy. Alone.'

The parents looked at each other.

'After all, it's *her* illness, not yours,' I pointed out. 'And under-sixteens are fully entitled to confidential consultations. Stop any lawyer and ask.'

Bill rose. He gripped Pam's shoulder. 'Come, my love, It is time we faced something – Gwen isn't going to be a child for ever.'

'I'll be brief,' I promised. 'Miss Brownlow must be fingering the Yamaha.' As the door shut, I asked, 'What about the pill, then?'

'Oh, that?' Gwen exclaimed in surprise. 'I'm off all that *absolutely*. Didn't you know? I heard last week I'd got a county hockey trial. Brill, isn't it?' She looked far more pleased than at the prospect of unfettered copulation. 'But of course, I can't risk any sort of emotional upset, can I? Not to mention draining my strength. Mrs Charrington says the whole of St Ursula's is proud of me, it's a terrif achievement, but I mustn't chance the slightest thing putting me off my game, not even catching a cold.'

I had the urge to bang my desk, tear my wisps of hair and shout, 'You stupid little twit! Don't you see my life's already exhausting enough, handling everyone's sore feet and arthritic hips and chronic sinuses and septic fingers and stiff necks and loose bowels? Why must you work out your sexual fantasies in my valuable time?'

Instead, I said, 'Very wise. I'm sure at your age you can get just as much fun from a vigorous bully-off.'

Amid all the changes and chances of twenty-five centuries, wrote Edwardian physician Sir William Osler, *the medical profession has never lacked men who have lived up to the Greek ideals.*

I felt faintly grateful to the Watsons. Any man enjoys awarding himself a medal for a battle in which nobody finally got hurt.

9

As Julius Caesar disliked the svelte, Sir Clifford Chatterley gamekeepers, and Ruth the alien corn, I dislike dinner parties.

'You're *abnormal*,' complained Sandra, putting down the telephone. 'Antisocial. Puritanical. Paranoic.'

I objected calmly, 'My own friends are enough trouble when they're pissed. I don't see why I should put up with other people's.'

'Well, I've accepted, anyway.'

'You haven't told me who it is?'

'The Haymasons.'

'Oh, that's completely different.'

It is as vulgar to discuss the food at a dinner party as the corpse at a funeral. This is a valuable social convention. For twenty-five years, Churchford has fed me a menu of prawns soaped with mayonnaise in an avocado hip bath, duck which has never taken to water and inelegant memorials to Pavlova. But Mrs Haymason's dishes opened such polite inhibitions like a deft oysterman's knife. Her dinner table expressed its delighted admiration of her cookery as uncontrollably as once the gallery at Drury Lane with Mrs Siddons' beauty.

'Cookery is part of the female erotic drive,' I reflected. I sat in our open-windowed living room with a glass of Talisker early on a warm May evening. 'Those fancy recipes in the Sunday supplements might make a man's mouth water, but Freud only suck his teeth. Those beautifully seductive photographs of goulash and gâteaux are quite as shameless as the pictures in multipostural sex manuals. It's the only way a woman can yield voluptuously to coarse male desires, now that sex is a rigorously equal activity, like a boxing match. And Mrs Haymason,' I reflected fondly, 'has a talent for the oven as Madame Pompadour for the bed.'

Rosemary Haymason was in her twenties, a softly bulging blonde, like a well-risen cheese soufflé.

'Any woman can become a culinary athlete by buying enough cookery books,' Sandra disagreed. 'There's almost as many in the shops as books on dieting.'

'No,' I mused. 'There's coquetry in tickling a man's palate as his other bits.' The clock struck. 'What's for dinner?'

'Steak and kidney pud.'

'There you are, then.'

'Any more of that and you won't get any,' said Sandra.

The Haymasons' lovely home stood in the costliest part of Churchford. The dinner party was Friday week, another sunny evening when its rowan-punctured avenues, prim with privet and tangy with lawn fertilizer, were lively with popping motor mowers, the teeth-gnashing of hedge clippers, the teasing chatter of cocktails on the patio.

Tim Haymason opened his front door, small, tidy, quiet, a property dealer, far richer in his thirties than I shall be in my dotage. His live-in Escoffier flitted in Habitat apron from her traditional rustic oak farmhouse kitchen, fully fitted with Neff ovens, microwaves and infrareds, spits and skillets, freezers and fish kettles, *moulins* and *mandolines*, herbarium and *hachoir*, whisks and woks.

As Rosemary tightly squeezed my arm, she whispered in my ear, 'Tonight you shall enjoy my gigot!' I felt it proved my point. She could have been referring to another part of her anatomy.

'Meet Adam and Deirdre.' Tim led us into his tasteful lounge.

It is intimidating, that first encounter with those you will sit among in conversational confinement as long as the Inter-City from London to Newcastle, and without the thematic diversion of the passing scenery. Adam was tall, fresh-faced, with curly brown hair and matching jacket. He wore sunglasses indoors. Deirdre was pale, skinny, her hair lank and dark. She said throatily, 'Hello.'

Tim announced respectfully, 'Adam knows absolutely everything about antiques.'

I embraced the couple with a smile. 'How pleasant for your wife, living with so many beautiful objects.'

'I can't answer for the beauty of the objects my wife lives with,' replied Adam, 'having just divorced her.'

'Ah!' Tim pressed a glass of Bruicladdich into my hand. 'And where do *you* live?' I asked Deirdre.

She seemed surprised. 'With Adam.'

I tried again. 'I don't expect you know this, but Rosemary's a fantastic cook.'

'Indeed, I do,' Adam replied weightily. 'I interviewed her for the gourmet column I write in *Home and Beauty*.'

'You're an expert on chips as well as Chippendale?'

He seemed puzzled. 'I don't think I follow?'

'Remarkably warm for May, isn't it?' said Sandra.

I suspected already that the evening might not be a success.

Adam's shop off the King's Road in Chelsea was called Lovely Things. He had met Rosemary the previous month, on a gourmet weekend organized by *Home and Beauty* at Périgueux ('The local *confit d'oie* is, of course, essential tasting, one relishes its earthiness like the robust charm of Le Nain's peasants one sees in the Louvre').

Deirdre worked at home for a Mayfair publisher, correcting authors' syntax ('Perfectly *illiterate* some of them'). This intellectual onslaught clearly fascinated and frightened Tim. His only artistic exercise was the imaginative descriptions of houses he hoped to sell for more than they were worth.

'*Rien ne dispose mieux l'esprit humain à des transactions amicales, qu'un dîner bien conçu et artistement préparé.*' Adam rubbed his podgy hands and tucked his napkin into his red check shirt as we sat round the sparkling dinner table. '*Telles réunions sont le berceau des bonnes moers et de la jovialité, comme la débauche est le tombeau de la moralité.* You see what I mean?' he invited all round.

Starters was raw monkfish marinated in vodka and red pepper.

'Those were, of course, the words of the famous Alexis Soyer,' Adam revealed.

'Florence Nightingale's chef at Scutari in the Crimean War,' I was able to contribute, but he took no notice.

'Original.' Adam inclined towards Rosemary after a forkful.

'Oh! You really think so?' she responded breathlessly.

'It inevitably recalls the Japanese sushi. But that must always be served with fresh seaweed. Home-made?' he inquired, cracking the crisp, eggshell-crusted brown roll.

Rosemary nodded eagerly. He savoured it, pursing his fleshy lips.

'Yes, you've got this just about right,' he conceded. 'It is the simple dishes one eats, barely noticing them, which express the fundamental skill of the cook. The analogy is Hepplewhite's joinery, you'll agree? Take the creation of the perfect omelette. The pan should be not only hot, but *smoking*.'

He expanded on the relative merits of Dijon and Meaux mustard, spaghetti *v.* macaroni, pigs' trotters or cow-heel, pickled onions and pappadums. Nobody else said anything except pass the butter.

The gigot appeared.

Adam took a mouthful and stared at the ceiling. 'Almost perfect.'

Rosemary gave a little squeal. 'You like it?'

He nodded gravely. She clapped her hands together. I noticed that Tim seemed off his food.

Adam expressed an opinion of gigot *d'agneau à la bonne femme* being superior to *à la bordelaise*, definitely to *à la boulangère*, and most certainly to *à la bretonne*. Deirdre seemed the quiet sort. I was preoccupied with the emetic properties of raw fish. Tim pushed his gigot aimlessly round his Limoges. Rosemary sat sparkle-eyed as Adam extended into gigot *persillé*, and *poêlé*. They might have been dining *tête-à-tête* in the candlelight. Then something frightful happened.

Tim thumped the table, rattling the Chambolle-Musigny '76. 'What's wrong with good old *à l'anglaise*?' he demanded.

We stared. He was usually as bland as a sago pudding.

'Indeed, served with clove-studded onions, a dish of charming naivety,' Adam conceded.

Rosemary dropped her glance into the *fonds d'artichauts farcis à la niçoise*. She gave a sob as gentle as a simmering *court-bouillon*. We sat in silence. Then we started sporadically munching, as people drift away from the scene of an accident. I had a sickening feeling. I was witnessing two men fighting for a woman with a leg of mutton.

Any dinner party is for the anxious hostess like a theatrical first night with the audience the cast. The Haymasons' ended undramatically, with the strawberry sorbet ('Entirely right – that delicious frosted pink of a Renoir nude'). We left early. Adam cornered me in the hall, slipped a card in my hand and murmured, 'If you're in the market for antiques, I'm competitive with anybody.'

That weekend was busy, on call for the practice. Early on Monday, Tim telephoned me at home. He wanted a consultation – in private. The epicurean Haymasons differed from the thespian Vaughans and the randy Watsons, who like many moneyed families in Churchford happily let their fellow-taxpayers fee their GP and give them each day their daily drugs. The National Health Service originated mercifully to provide the poor with an alternative to the grave. It now conveniently provides the middle classes with the alternative to a new car.

Tim appeared at the surgery that evening. He had bellyache.

'Like wolves gnawing my inside,' he explained nervously.

'For how long?' I asked.

'About a month, since Rosemary's *foie gras* trip.' He hesitated. 'I'm a complicated case. It could wreck my marriage.'

'Oh, tut,' I objected. 'I've seen marriages ruined by alcoholism but never by indigestion.'

'Don't you realize, doctor? The first thing that attracted me to Rosemary was Katie Stewart's family cooking.' He looked dreamy, still holding his stomach. 'How I remember, we honeymooned on Elizabeth David's French provincial! I've cherished Rosemary through all her moods – Delia Smith, Constance Spry, Robert Carrier, even Fanny Craddock. But if I can't digest – say, her braised guinea-fowl with figs, her lambs' tongues casseroled in cider, her goat-cheese rarebit – she'll soon find someone else who can,' he ended miserably.

'Oh, come come!' I remonstrated. 'Oh, pooh pooh! There's more to marriage than four bare legs in bed or two pairs of knives and forks on a table.'

He shifted uneasily in the patient's chair. 'I know, the basic recipe is love, sympathy, companionship, all that. But marriages are made in Heaven with some special ingredient. Maybe a mutual interest, anything from the garden to the children. Rosemary's never managed to get a bun in the oven, so cookery's a big slice of her life.' He asked diffidently, 'Do you suppose I could have a second opinion?'

With a gastroenterologist or a psychiatrist? I wondered. I recommended Gerry Gravelston at the General. 'He knows more about the gut than the tapeworm,' I assured the patient.

10

Tim's appointment with the stomach consultant came the following Monday. I was finishing evening surgery when he telephoned Mrs Jenkins asking me to call urgently. This was worrying. I had made my diagnosis – dyspepsia caused by his worry over Rosemary fancying Adam. Had Gerry Gravelston found something more sinister? A peptic ulcer? An acute gallbladder? Had I mishandled the case? Had I eaten Tim's salt only to rub it into his wounds?

Tim greeted me gravely at the front door. On the peony-patterned four-seater settee with frilled valence in the elegant lounge sat Rosemary and Adam, looking serious.

'Well!' I rubbed my hands. Nobody spoke. 'Well, well! And how was our consultation?'

'I am dying,' Tim announced.

'What? Why? How? You?' I exclaimed. 'Did Dr Gravelston announce thus?'

'No,' said Tim.

'Then what the hell gave you the bright idea?' I demanded.

'I could see it in his eyes.'

'Really!' I lost patience. 'Don't be barmy. That's his bedside manner. He's known throughout the trade as "Graveyard" Gravelston. He'd look exactly the same if he heard he'd won the pools during a weekend with Bo Derek in Bali.'

Tim stuck his hands in his pockets and walked the Afghan rug. 'It's only a matter of time before someone pushes the button on me in the crematorium.'

'How's the pain?' I inquired.

'Now it's like hungry jackals feeding.'

'I bet Dr Gravelston's official report says your stomach would be the envy of a flock of ostriches,' I encouraged him.

'I want you to know something, doctor,' Tim pronounced. 'After the unfortunate event of my death, Adam has – most considerately – agreed to take care of Rosemary.'

I was puzzled. 'You mean, by executing your will?'

He raised a smile as insubstantial as a plate of profiteroles. 'In the fullest sense. I cannot bear to think of anyone as wonderful as Rosemary alone in the world.'

Adam and Rosemary exchanged reverent glances. They slowly reached out and held hands.

'She is so charming, so modest, so defenceless,' Tim continued in a low voice. 'Yet with her heavenly gifts! For an art respected everywhere from palaces to prisons.'

'Gasterea is the tenth Muse,' Adam recited solemnly. 'The delights of taste are her domain. The whole world would be hers if she wished to claim it. For the world is nothing without life, and all that lives takes nourishment. Brillat-Savarin,' he enlightened us. I thought him decent to give it in translation.

'I can die in peace, knowing that with Adam she will be absolutely fulfilled in all departments,' Tim declared.

'But you're going to live,' I insisted, 'to consume countless steaks unborn and vintages yet uncrushed.'

'I am but a common property dealer,' he confessed miserably. 'I have no pretensions to be arty or intellectual. I simply enjoy things with my body – food, pictures, music, the spring flowers, and the, you know, doctor. But Rosemary is more sensitive. Her emotions have an aesthetic dimension. Adam was saying so when you came in.'

Adam rose. He gripped Tim's hands. 'It is a trust comparable with custody of the Holy Grail.'

Rosemary rose. She kissed Adam lightly on the cheek. She kissed Tim lightly on the cheek. She burst into tears. She sobbed on Adam's shoulder, then on Tim's. I wished to leave. They were all nutters.

'I have an urgent call to the St Boniface Twilight Home,' I announced.

Rosemary damply transferred herself to me. 'Do stay,' she choked, 'and enjoy my poussin.'

'I'm sure you've got enough for anyone who fancies a slice,' I thanked her. 'But I've my own boiled beef and carrots at home. I implore you – roll up the blueprint until I've heard from Dr Gravelston. Good evening.'

His letter was in the surgery three mornings later. I telephoned Tim at once.

'Caught you over the croissants?' I greeted him cheerfully. 'Good news! No organic cause for your dyspepsia.'

'My what?' He appeared puzzled. 'Oh, you mean that tummy upset? I'd almost forgotten about it, I must say. Kind of you to take such trouble.'

He was a changed man. I was mystified. I asked how he felt.

'Absolutely fine! Super! Terrific. I could eat anything – curry, haggis, hot lobster, stewed biltong. Bring your dear lady to dinner this evening.'

I demurred. He insisted. I agreed. It would be interesting to observe the cure. And a man can never enjoy too many birthdays or good dinners. Also, I remembered it was cottage-pie night at home.

Sandra and I drove to the Haymasons.

I rang Tim's bell with the salivating expectation of Bertie Wooster arriving at Brinkley Court to browse at the trough of Aunt Dahlia, employer of chef Anatole, that superb master of the roasts and hashes (her dyspeptic husband once insanely tried swapping him for an eighteenth-century cow-creamer).

It was not Rosemary who opened the door, but Deirdre.

'Hel*lo*,' she said.

With a cheerful shout, Tim bounded in in a butcher's apron from the kitchen, wooden spoon in one hand, fish slice in the other. 'The Krug's on ice,' he announced heartily.

'Rosemary would seem to have thrown in the dishcloth,' observed Sandra, as the cork popped in the lounge.

'Rosemary?' Tim seemed to have forgotten her like his bellyache. 'You remember, doctor, how Adam was to comfort Rosemary after my death? As everything was cut and dried, there seemed no point in awaiting my blast-off to Heaven. So Rosemary's moved in with Adam.' He poured the champagne. 'Which left Deirdre at a loose end. So she came along to pass the time with me. You can correct authors' syntax anywhere. Deirdre, love, there's a peculiar smell from the kitchen, would you take a look? If anything's on fire, there's an extinguisher in the garage.'

My smouldering unease burst into panic. '*You're* cooking dinner?'

Tim nodded enthusiastically. 'Nothing to it. I'm amazed how Rosemary could make a meal into something like raising the *Titanic*. Living with a skillet expert, Deirdre hasn't brandished a loaded saucepan for months,' he explained. 'Not that I believe she was ever your actual Mrs Beeton, she was more into hamburgers and Yorkie bars. *Was* anything burning?' he asked, as she slipped back like a chilly shadow.

'It was only the fat again.'

'I'm giving you my moussaka,' Tim announced proudly. It tasted like Irish stew made with engine oil. I pushed the nauseous mess round my plate. Sandra picked at the accompanying baked beans. Deirdre busied herself with the packet of sliced bread and packet of butter. Tim scoffed his with the horrifying avidity of Moloch getting through a nursery school. Luckily, he had opened several bottles of the Gevry-Chambertin '72. Once Deirdre had yawned and said vibrantly. 'Bed*time*,' we left.

'Food,' I mused, as Sandra drove home. 'How more significant than nutrition! Gluttony is dignified as a cardinal sin. Starvation is cruelty without scars. Food has its diseases – anorexia from eating too little, bulimia from eating too much. The ageless fear of hunger has been replaced by the terror of obesity. People waste money on food which they hope will make them healthy, even on oysters which they hope will make someone else randy. Food can inspire magnificent art, particularly among Dutchmen.'

'You're rambling,' said Sandra.

'Did you know that André Maurois once wrote a story about food? Among his imaginary Erophagi hunger replaced sex, with all its passions and taboos. Couples ate secretly, but invited friends to come and make love as we invite them to dinner. It makes my Freudian point.'

'*This* stew is nothing but old-fashioned wife-swapping,' said Sandra firmly. 'It's always happening in Churchford, men taking a fancy to housewives all tarted up and tanked up at dinner parties. Fairly pointless,

I'd say – they all behave with exactly the same lack of originality across the tablecloth as they doubtless do between the sheets.'

'I wonder if we've the end of that veal and ham pie left in the fridge?' I speculated.

The following Monday evening, Rosemary appeared in my consulting room.

'I've made a terrible mistake,' she began miserably.

'Adam? Gone sour?'

'He won't let me into his kitchen.'

'When George Sand moved in with Chopin, he probably wouldn't let her touch his piano,' I suggested consolingly.

'But cooking is my whole *life*,' she said anguishedly. 'And he won't even allow me to make the tea.'

'But surely you can enjoy his own beautiful cooking? Only someone like you can appreciate it profoundly. Great critics are honoured as much as the great artists they admire,' I pointed out.

'Ug!' She shuddered. 'He's going through his Russian phase. All coulibiaca and *bilini*. Fish pie and pancakes. I've nothing to do all day except sit in his nasty Battersea flat filled with out-of-date furniture – not a bit what I'm used to, Tim insisted I went to the Ideal Home Exhibition every year – and Adam's incredibly fussy about scratches and rings, he says everything has to go back to the shop. I can't even enjoy cookery books, it's like reading travel guides in jail. Do you know how I really feel?' She looked at me wide-eyed. 'Like a respectable wife seduced from a good, decent, adoring husband by a glamorous lover who turns out to be a useless, unresponsive homosexual.'

'Why not drive straight home, go into the kitchen and start knocking up an entrecôte *à la béarnaise* for Tim's dinner?'

'What, with that dreadful woman there?' she exclaimed in horror. 'You can't imagine some of the peculiar things she's left behind in Battersea.'

I sighed. The setting of fractured marriages are tricky cases for GPs. But I promised tactful overtures to Tim. Anything to avoid the possibility of more moussaka.

Two mornings later he appeared unannounced in the surgery, as miserable as Rosemary.

'The pain, doctor.'

'Worse?'

He clutched his midriff. 'I might have been eating barbed-wire bolognese.'

'You're still doing the cooking?'

He shook his head. 'Deirdre complained it was inedible. So she took over the kitchen, but can't produce anything except egg, chips and peas. They don't seem to agree with me. I just sit at the table remembering the lovely meals Rosemary used to lavish on me.'

I put my fingertips together. 'I suspect your trouble, Tim, is not what you're getting your teeth into.'

He looked puzzled. 'Oh, you mean...? Well, yes, in fact you're right.' He looked relieved. 'Deirdre's a lovely girl, very cultured, she knows an awful lot about syntax, but frankly, I thought she was a bombe *surprise* when she's only a portion of bone stew.'

'The old story,' I remarked consolingly. 'The spinach is always greener on the other man's plate.'

'What am I going to do?' he asked pathetically. 'Consult the Marriage Guidance Council or the *Good Food Guide*?'

'Leave it to your doctor,' I said smugly. 'I think I can arrange to put you all back to square one, or to the hors d'oeuvres if you prefer it.'

He was touchingly grateful. 'Particularly,' he added, shaking hands, 'as Deirdre has some very strange habits about the house.'

The piecrust was broken, the birds could begin to sing. I make a telephone call to Battersea. The following week, the Haymasons invited us to dinner.

'I've cooked up a brilliant idea to solve our emotional difficulties,' Tim announced happily, upending the second empty Bollinger into the ice bucket as we sat at the table. 'Rosemary's unbelievable talents are just being wasted, with only me at home to enjoy them. No wonder she's so frustrated. But I've got my hands on a bit of property in South Ken, and she's opening a restaurant,' he revealed proudly.

'Fantastic, isn't it?' asked Rosemary, bright-eyed. 'For years I've been giving such pleasure to my friends for free. Why not take it up professionally?'

I agreed heartily. I did not mention that exactly the same argument applied to prostitution.

Freud and I were right. Cookery absorbs a housewife's sex urge as devotion a nun's, power a politician's, contemplation a mystic's and football a schoolboy's. A woman steaming only over a hot stove contributes admirably to the stability of family life and our national morality. For what we are about to receive, I reflected, starting my *oeufs en gelée à l'estragon*, the Lord may be truly thankful.

The dinner was superb.

If food be the music of love, give me excess of it.

11

My privilege of saving their lives is restricted to the $12^1/_2$ per cent of my patients who suffer from acute major illness. (I did not work this out. The Department of Health and Social Security have men to do it at the Elephant and Castle, set tunefully in London between the Old Kent Road and the Lambeth Walk.)

Twenty-five per cent have chronic illness. I help carry their kit as they soldier on through life.

The rest the Department labels 'minor illnesses' – though there are neither minor illnesses nor minor operations to a patient. Every man is of supreme importance to himself, as I expect Dr Johnson said.

Five per cent come with 'emotional disorders'. If I am criticized for countering these with drugs, I am responding in the way I was trained to a condition I should not be treating. This is pastoral medicine, better handled by the vicar. But the Church has sadly lost the clinical touch since its splendid work in the Black Death. The nation floats on a sea of tranquillity, preferring chemical to spiritual relief as speedier and risking neither censure of its sins nor the necessity to stop committing them.

When Syd Farthingale appeared in the surgery one early summer morning, I suspected the emotional was masked by the physical. Patients often offer one disability as an excuse for introducing another – girls with palpitations are pregnant, stockbrokers have not constipation but clap.

'I find absolutely no sign of these rheumatics you're complaining of, Mr Farthingale,' I assured him weightily.

He folded his arms reflectively. He was short, fat, pale and puffy, sparse dark hair arranged economically across his scalp. He was a man of

Napoleonic power. At the General Hospital he was shop steward for the Association of Confederated Health Employees (ACHE), whose complicated disagreement with his rival shop stewards for General Ancillary Services Personnel (GASP) and the Organization for Unqualified Co-operatives in Health (OUCH) over deploying the new electrical floor cleaners had earlier kept the General's brand-new Elizabeth Wing empty and idle for months.

Once, Syd Farthingale decided which patients might be admitted, when surgeons might operate, whether the wards might have hot dinners and the beds clean sheets, whether dirty refuse or dead humans were properly disposed of. He had cowed the Royal College of Nursing, ignored the TUC, infuriated the BMA and exasperated the government. But the national climate had cyclically softened from its winters of discontent. Syd Farthingale had not met his Waterloo, but he was taking a sabbatical on St Helena.

I wondered if this slow puncture of the ego was affecting his psychological suspension. 'Any other reason for your feeling tense, anxious, nervous?'

He announced, 'Well, actually, I got this bodyscanner.'

I suggested, 'Perhaps we have our terminology in a twist? A bodyscanner is a machine, not a complaint.'

'I mean this bodyscanner what I got in my front room.'

I raised my eyebrows. 'What an extraordinary article to have about the house! Surely they don't put them in those mail-order catalogues, like the sandwich toasters?'

He glanced round furtively. 'Look, doctor. This is all between four walls, innit?'

I raised my right hand and informed him smugly, ' "Whatever I see or hear, professionally or privately, which ought not to be divulged, I will keep secret and tell no one." Hippocratic Oath. Looked it up again only yesterday.' (Crossword clue.)

Syd Farthingale asked warily, 'I mean, the Old Bill ain't arriving to copy my medical file into their notebooks?'

'Even if the Lord Chancellor blew in, he wouldn't get a butcher's.'

Folding his arms again, he remarked, 'You know what hospitals are these days, doctor. Everything disposable.'

I nodded. 'Cheaper than washing up.'

'So there's a lot of stuff lying around. Stands to reason. Paper operating hats, used needles, old scalpels, plastic razors, rubber gloves, wipes. Doing them a favour, arni?'

I was puzzled. 'How?'

'Carting it all away, o'course,' he explained patiently. 'Why, I'm probably saving the Health Service thousands a year in refuse collection. Do I get thanks for it? No, I do not! And the way the government's carrying on about pinching every penny, I ask you. These crates were lying about in the stores a couple of years, no one seemed to want them, so I disposed of them.'

'Crates? What crates?'

'The ones in the stores,' he spelt out. 'We used my mate Len's van what delivers the patients' flowers. Get them home, find they contain a bodyscanner. Diabolical.'

'I see. You're worried at stealing an essential piece of hospital equipment.'

'Not thieving, doctor, if you don't mind,' he replied indignantly, 'just saving space. It's shocking the General couldn't put to merciful use this scanner, saving human lives and that. No, they say, we have no money to pay staff to work it, similar with six wards and a new block of operating theatres. The government don't give a monkey's if people die in the streets.'

'The financing of the National Health Service presents many difficulties, certainly,' I agreed.

'But I meantersay, what can I do with a bleeding bodyscanner?' Syd Farthingale dropped political arguments. 'I cannot flog it in a pub, like a load of syringes – all disposed-of ones, of course, doctor. I cannot sell it for scrap, like them obsolescent operating tables what they got hanging about the stores last year. I cannot get rid of it through the trade, like five thousand gallons of paint what was ordered the wrong colour. Nobody's got the welfare of the General nearer their heart than me, doctor, I don't mind clearing away their unwanted goods, but who'd work for nothing?

Can you help a bloke?' he ended, as miserably as Napoleon performing a U-turn at Moscow.

'Mr Farthingale, I cannot approve of your business methods, but I should like to see the scanner back at the General on the off chance that one day somebody might possibly use it,' I told him primly. 'Surely the simplest remedy for a complex piece of scientific apparatus in your parlour, doubtless dreadfully awkward when you have friends round for a jar, is to replace it in the flower van, back up to the door of the storeroom, and put it back?'

'There's a snag, doctor. You see, Len's doing a bit of porridge. It was a misunderstanding. Someone was using his credit card.'

'Nothing criminal in that,' I objected, mystified.

'And vice versa,' he explained. 'You see, we nicked this bodyscanner at Christmas. No one at the General's noticed yet. Mind, I reckon they'll take as long to start wanting it back as them Greeks with the Elgin marbles what we borrowed. But you never know, some people are always inquisitive,' he mused. 'Though mind you, if the fuzz sledge-hammered down my front door looking for things, I'd have the lads out at the General in a pig's whisper. Bring the healing process to a grinding halt, police harassment, innit? The same with spares going missing from British Leyland, you name it, meantersay, the law has no place in industrial relations, right?'

'I have a brilliant idea.'

He sat up and stared like Napoleon at Marshal Ney clearing his throat at the council table.

When entangled in the genito-gastric complex of the hedonistic Haymasons, I had recalled a tale about feeding substituting for fornicating, written by the Frenchman André Maurois (who ended up writing the biography of Alexander Fleming). Searching then for the story in the bookshelf, I had discovered it in his *Silence of Colonel Bramble*, a sentimental, sad, sycophantically satirical image of the British in World War One – and so in all wars from the Hundred Years' to our next one, a nation's character changing only as slowly as the modulations of Darwinism.

Colonel Bramble embodied a story about another colonel, who commands an ammunition depot. One morning, he discovers only forty-nine machine guns, not fifty. To spare himself unending trouble with the War Office, perhaps his pay stopped, possibly a court martial, the wily officer indents for the replacement of a broken machine-gun tripod, which is sent without question. The next month for a replacement gun sight, then ammunition feed, recoil plate, trigger assembly, until by his retirement from the Army he had reconstructed an entire machine gun.

I felt the principle could be applied in reverse to the weapons of life.

'Why not leave the bodyscanner round the hospital in bits?' I suggested. 'No one will look twice at you, taking a computer or whatever from the boot of your car, carrying it through the front door and dropping it in the canteen or outpatients'. The law can't put a finger on you, once you've restored the *status quo ante*, even in fragments.'

He was awestruck. 'I wish I had your brains, doctor.'

I held up a hand again. ' "Calm deliberation unravels every knot." Harold Macmillan. He hung it up in Downing Street.'

The bodyscanner vanished from my mind as entirely as from the storeroom. I was confident that a man of Syd Farthingale's subtlety, who could halt the General's operating by blacking the laundering of the surgeons' white trousers, would effortlessly free himself from his electronic incubus.

The following week, we were invited to dinner by the Windrushes. He is a pathologist at the General, a tall, sinewy man whom I tolerate as a golfing companion despite his painful medical-student sense of humour. Over the inescapable roast frozen duck, I inquired idly, 'Is there much thieving at the hospital?'

He guffawed. 'You must be joking. Don't you know, the National Health Service is Britain's Sin City? Makes Chicago look like Lourdes.'

I had an irrational but irrepressible uneasiness.

'They nick anything from X-ray films for the silver and oxygen cylinders for the steel, to the patients' flowers and toffees. Mad, coming into hospital with any money, wristwatch, soap, even clothes. Government sheets, pillowcases, towels, nighties, you could open a branch of Marks and Spencer's. Detergent, floor polish, it's all on the invoices, but it's fairy gold for someone. The canteens lose millions in swiped chicken legs, cheese rolls and suchlike; with the money the government could open half the wards it closed for economy. Did you hear about our bodyscanner?'

I dropped my knife and fork.

'Didn't Jilly tell you? Enormous row at the General. It was whipped. Out of the stores. Not even unpacked.'

'Utterly, appallingly cruel.' His wife shuddered.

'I don't know what the world's coming to.' So did mine.

'Worse still,' Windrush continued with relish, 'it was donated by the Friends of Man, the do-gooder lot, the fruit of people giving themselves coronaries on marathons, diverting good beer money into pub collecting boxes, free-falling from aeroplanes and playing the piano for twenty-four hours, you know the thing. Naturally, they're making a terrific fuss. Man's Best Friend was down, enormous bloke in a prickly green suit, beard like a fretful porpentine, pulverizing Applebee the administrator.' Windrush stared at me. 'You all right, Richard? You've turned white.'

'Just a touch of the old dyspepsia.'

He grinned. 'I thought you might have the bodyscanner in your front room, or something.'

'I do hope you'll be able to enjoy the Pavlova,' said Mrs Windrush considerately.

That night I confided to Sandra about Syd Farthingale.

'I'd have reported him to the police,' she said firmly.

'How could I? Professional secrecy. Hippocratic Oath.'

'Pooh! A man like Farthingale would have stolen Aesculapius' staff and serpents and sold them as kebabs.'

'They'll find the scanner round the hospital,' I suggested hopefully, 'decide there was a mix-up with the equipment, and see if anyone's been trying to make a diagnosis with a canteen toaster. I expect the fuss will die down.'

The fuss had as little chance of dying down as the one about Burke and Hare.

12

'The General's in trouble again,' Mrs Jenkins greeted me when I arrived at the surgery two mornings later. 'Worse than that time the old operating-theatre ceiling caved in.'

She passed me Britain's most popular paper, with SCANNER SCANDAL! on the front page. Outraged, it recounted a miracle machine presented to the government by saintly citizens, only to be lost by the National Health Service as casually as a commuter's umbrella. The paper expressed little wonder at doctors continually cutting off the wrong arms and legs and leaving the cutlery inside.

I painfully feigned amused detachment. The case of the misplaced scanner was hardly my responsibility, but I had the feeling of not wishing to encounter Syd Farthingale again any more than Her Majesty might welcome intruders in her bedroom.

He appeared at evening surgery.

'What about putting it back?' I started sternly.

'But doctor, I *have* put it back,' he replied nervously. 'Every bleeding bit of it, it's all round the hospital, everywhere from the consultants' toilet to the mortuary. Been there all week, but nobody seems to notice,' he complained indignantly. 'It's amazing! People are blind. I suppose there's always bits and pieces hanging about hospitals, you know, sort of wheelchairs, laundry bins, cardiac-arrest trolleys, everyone thinks it's someone else's job to shift them. It's on my conscience, doctor, something terrible.'

'So it should be,' I told him harshly.

'I mean, all this in the papers, kids giving up their pocket money and that.'

'I'm glad you feel the extent of your heartlessness.'

'Also, Mr Applebee the administrator – no pal of mine, I'm telling you – is beginning to ask questions like, Have I got anything that dropped off the back of an ambulance? Pure victimization. And furthermore,' he admitted miserably, 'the lads ain't all that solid on police harassment; in fact, if they saw the police harassing me they'd probably all fall about. I dunno, the old spirit's gone since those days when you'd get Mr Applebee on bended knee asking me please to turn the water on again. I just don't know what to do next.'

'Let me make it crystal clear, Mr Farthingale, that I utterly refuse to become involved with this sordid affair further.'

'But you got to help me, doctor,' he insisted.

I gave the look of Dr Arnold at Rugby selecting the right birch for the stroke. 'Go to Mr Applebee first thing tomorrow and make a clean breast of it.'

'I'd like to, doctor. But what about you?'

'Me?'

'Well, it's you what suggested it,' he said slyly. 'We're in this together, ain't we?'

I was aghast. 'You…you own up at once,' I proposed weakly.

'Then there's these other things.'

'What other things?'

'Well, sort of pyjamas, sets of operating instruments, towels, dressings, soap, crates of sugar and tea, few washing machines, typewriters, beds, gowns, gloves, sets of canteen trays, speculums, sigmoidoscopes, packs of razors, anaesthetic machines, cornflakes; the wife's for ever complaining there's hardly room to swing a cat, and that's come from the General, too.'

'You must take it all back,' I told him, flustered. 'At once. Rent a van. An articulated lorry, if necessary.'

'Supposing there was a spot of bother with the Old Bill?' He eyed me like Napoleon observing the Imperial Guard charge an unexpected breech in the enemy's lines. 'They'd feel real puzzled you never grassed, wouldn't they? So's they could call on me early one morning and make a nice clean job of it. They got shockingly suspicious minds, the police. That's perverting the course of justice, innit? Funny thing,' he reminisced, 'a pal of mine got done for just that last Whitsun. Matter of getting a witness to suffer what you doctors call loss of memory. Got six years. Mind, the judge was a silly old moo, got the idea in his head that witnesses tell the truth actual. Come to think of it,' he speculated knowledgeably, 'the law might have you and me for conspiracy, then there's no limit to the sentence, not so's you notice it.'

Mr Farthingale,' I said. 'If you are ill, I shall be delighted to see you any time of the day or night. If you are not, I never want to see you again. Ever. Good evening.'

I drove to the General as soon as surgery was over. Jilly was finishing an operating list. She emerged from the theatre in pale blue operating dress, paper hat and white clogs, clipboard of patient's notes under her arm.

'Why, Daddy,' she greeted me cheerfully. 'Seeing a patient?'

'Do you know a man called Farthingale?'

Jilly nodded vigorously. 'Yes, one of the theatre porters, and cheeky with it. I've a vague feeling he may not be completely honest.'

'Something terrible has happened.' I grasped her bare forearm. 'I see myself struck off the register, disgraced, dishonoured, disowned, arrested, tried. I hear the clang of prison doors. I shall have to resign from the golf club.'

'Golly,' said Jilly.

'I must talk.'

'Well, I must see a patient in recovery. Look, go down to the mess. I'll come and buy you a drink,' she suggested charitably.

And what would Dr Quaggy say? I wondered. That I was Churchford's answer to Dr Crippen?

I put the case to her in the residents' bar.

'But why don't you run and tell a policeman?' she asked, mystified. 'There's always plenty of them hanging about accident and emergency.'

I explained desperately. 'That would be simply clapping my own handcuffs, as the ghastly little ponce's accomplice.'

'But the police would always accept your word for what happened.'

'They didn't when I drove into that milk float.'

'I know! Turn Queen's evidence. Then you can lay it on as thick as you like.'

'There's more than legal quibbles,' I explained in martyred tones. 'He can sneak on me, but I can't on him. Unethical, you see. Professional secrecy. I learned about the scanner only as the cause of his psychological disturbance. It would be exactly the same if he'd asked me to treat a gunshot wound, or bellyache from gulping a handful of diamonds before going through Customs. Hippocrates really does choose the most awkward times to come whispering in your ear.'

'Oh, come off it, Daddy. All you'd get from the GMC would be a round of applause. Why, hello, Dr Windrush.'

I grabbed him by the lapels. He was too alarmed even for his usual humourless remark about rich GPs buying penniless pathologists a drink. I repeated my evidence. He gave a low whistle. 'Well, breaking stones every day in broad arrows is a jolly sight healthier exercise than jogging in a sexy tracksuit –'

'You've got to help me.'

'Don't worry, they'll probably give you a cushy job in the library, with the stockbrokers and defrocked clergymen –'

'You have got to help my father,' said Jilly fiercely.

He looked startled. 'Sorry. I only came to collect a specimen from a houseman, but I'll have a gin and ton. Perhaps we should send Applebee an anonymous letter saying where the bits of scanner are, like a treasure hunt? He's a dreadful creep, of course, no more than a frustrated VAT inspector, but this affair has dropped him so deep in the droppings, he'd be too grateful to fuss how the thing came to be scattered under his nose. He can organize search parties, issue a statement to the press that the scanner was merely mislaid, something that's always happening in government departments. I mean, the Foreign Office is for ever leaving top-secret papers in bistros, the Army litters Dorset with unexploded shells, and the Exchequer loses millions of quid every time it tries to add up.'

'Without mentioning that king-sized kleptomaniac Farthingale?' I asked.

'No need. I'll say it came to me in a dream.'

A ray of sunlight fell between the iron-studded gates. 'I wouldn't mind seeing Farthingale get his just deserts,' I reflected warmly. 'Preferably stuffed up somewhere uncomfortable.'

'Leave it to me,' said Windrush, sipping thoughtfully.

That night I could barely sleep. I kept listening for the Old Bill sledge-hammering down my front door. After morning surgery, I missed lunch and drove to the General.

I bleeped Jilly. She was with Mr Applebee, and would I come up? I took the lift to the administration floor. Approaching down the corridor was Windrush.

'Richard! I've fixed that one-man Mafia, Farthingale,' he greeted me cheerfully. 'Grabbed him in the porters' rest room – where he earns his pay playing pontoon – said he'd been shopped, demanded to know where the loot was stashed, and said I'd see he collected ten years unless he resigned as shop steward of ACHE. I got really tough, made Judge Jeffreys look like a social worker. Don't you see? This'll instantly reopen the children's ward, closed because of his row with the shop steward of OUCH about who'll screw in the light bulbs, or something. I'm just bearing the good news to Applebee. He'll be over the moon, won't think of asking nasty questions. By the way, your Jilly's been scavenging. Oh, Applebee's having a wonderful morning.'

Jilly was in the office amid a bodyscanner assembly kit. Applebee was a small man with thick dark hair, thick dark-rimmed glasses and a well-pressed dark suit. He was standing behind his desk beating his brow with the palm of his hand and shouting hysterically, 'This is the end!'

Jilly gave a little wave. 'You know our Mr Applebee?'

'The end!' he repeated.

'Something the matter?' murmured Windrush.

'Look at this!' Applebee flourished a flimsy. 'The scanner I indented from the Department of Health five years ago. It's arrived. This morning. It's in crates, down in the storeroom. I still cannot afford to run one scanner. What the hell am I going to do with two?'

'Send it back,' Windrush pointed out.

Applebee gave a high-pitched laugh. 'Send it back? Impossible! You know what they'd do? Dock my budget. Then I'd have to close another operating theatre. I think I shall resign,' he ended miserably.

'The administration of the National Health Service presents many difficulties, certainly,' I agreed.

RICHARD GORDON

'I know!' suggested Jilly. 'Take the new one to London, and distribute it in bits round the Department headquarters at the Elephant and Castle.'

But Applebee did not seem to possess even a VAT man's sense of humour. His voice broke. 'I never want to see another hospital. I'm going to tear up my kidney donor card.'

I laughed loudly.

Everyone stared.

'I've just remembered! The colonel commanding that ammunition depot ended up with fifty-one machine guns. Dreadfully embarrassing. Took years to get rid of the extra one again.'

'What machine guns?' asked Applebee sharply.

'Oh, the colonel in the story. The one that gave me the idea of telling Syd Farthingale to put the scanner back on the sly, when he confessed to me in the surgery two weeks ago that he'd stolen it.'

'What's all this?' glared Applebee.

'Oh, Daddy,' sighed Jilly.

'Oh, Daddy!' grinned Windrush.

'Mr Applebee,' said Jilly. 'You've had a trying time. Let's go down to the residents' bar, shall we, where my father will stand us all drinks.'

13

Windrush telephoned during breakfast.

'Syd Farthingale?' I said at once. 'Applebee's had him arrested? Or had the sense to give him a job? Equipment procurement officer, the most economical one in the Health Service.'

'I am calling to congratulate you.'

I asked on what.

'Your election as president of the Churchford Cricket Club.'

I was stumped.

'It was decided last night at the club's annual general meeting, after dinner at the Blue Boar.'

I pointed out, 'But I'm not a member of the Churchford Cricket Club.'

'Then the greater the honour.'

'But it's ridiculous! I don't know anything about cricket. I've only been to Lord's once, and it rained all day. Everyone got terribly drunk.'

'The consensus of the meeting was to bestow the distinction on a widely respected, indeed beloved, GP. You're not being very gracious, nitpicking like this.'

Windrush can be overbearing, I suppose through his job as a pathologist of continually facing fellow-doctors with their mistakes.

He added emolliently, 'All the president does is sit in a deckchair in the sun while the batting side keep bringing him pints of hitter. And you know who you're replacing?' I warily recognized his wily voice, in which he made helpful suggestions when we played golf. 'The biggest cricket buff in Churchford. Bill Ightam, your daughter Jilly's chief at the General.'

I hesitated. Surgical eminence is like sainthood achieved through finite steps of increasing radiance. Jilly had risen from houseman to Bill Ightam's registrar. Her ascent to senior registrar depended on the sort of reference he wrote her.

'Good, you've accepted!' said Windrush forcefully. 'Congratulations. I'll drop into your house, to present you with your club tie.'

'Aren't you a little senior for schoolboy games?' Sandra suggested, when I explained this at the kitchen breakfast table.

'It's more than a game, it's a national institution,' I corrected her. 'The Men of Hambledon are as much a part of our history as the Tolpuddle Martyrs. They played cricket in Dickens – Dingley Dell *v.* the All-Muggletons – and surely you remember there's a breathless hush in the Close tonight, play up! play up! play up! and play the game! Why, the most famous cricketer who ever went to the crease was a doctor.'

I already felt the dignity of office.

I finished my tomato omelette with grilled tomatoes. It was a Thursday morning in June, when my long evenings were spent in the greenhouse. This was set against the southern wall of our Victorian villa, facing St Alphege's (vicar low church and low back pain). It was a Christmas present from Sandra, as a tranquillizer. Like my patients, it had endured a winter battle against infection – mealy bug, leaf miner, thrips, wireworms – which I similarly treated with powerful chemicals until it was more sterile than the operating theatres at the General, where Jilly tells me the problem of cross-infection is worse than that of surgical egos.

In June the greenhouse became as rewarding as the end of a multiple pregnancy, cucumbers dangling as plump as green salami, aubergines as burstingly purple as nasty bruises, tomatoes pressing against the panes like commuters crammed into rush-hour trains. That morning, I had proudly presented Sandra with my first trug of Ailsa Craigs.

My shrewdness in accepting the presidency was emphasized during the day by my partner Dr Elaine Spondeck, who recounted that Dr Quaggy was desperate for the honour.

'Local prestige, you know, which he confuses with personal advancement,' I told Sandra that evening. 'One in the eye for him, eh?'

I set two piled trugs on the kitchen table, where she was making our spaghetti *al pomodoro*.

'Tomatoes,' she murmured.

'Yes, I'm going to need a machete to hack my way in soon,' I said enthusiastically. 'I think it's transfusing the Gro-bags with stale blood. Tomatoes just love getting their roots into juicy human haemoglobin.'

'Perhaps I can do stuffed tomatoes for tomorrow's lunch,' she said doubtfully. 'And tomatoes *à la parisienne* for dinner. I suppose it's always nice to lay down a shelf of tomato chutney.'

The doorbell rang. It was Windrush, flourishing my tie. I thanked him, remarking that the purple and pink stripes went surprisingly well with the primrose.

'Did I mention on the phone yesterday about the donation?'

'Of course, I should be delighted.' I generously mooted a sum.

'Come off it, Richard,' he complained ungratefully. 'This isn't a kid's playgroup. It's our long-standing tradition that the president donates heftily. As we're badly in the red, I'd rather appreciate the cheque here and now. And you might make a note in your diary of the club's annual dinner,' he directed. 'First Saturday in October, Blue Boar, big do. We always get some first-class cricketer for the speech, maybe Botham, Mike Brearley, Geoff Boycott. To the president falls the honour of introducing him – you don't mind?'

'Charmed.'

'Also of paying his fee, hotel and travelling expenses.'

'Fine! While we're at it, why not invite Lillee or Rod Marsh across from Australia?'

But Windrush is as insensitive to irony as traffic wardens to imprecation.

'You're attending our local Derby on Saturday v. Beagle Hill?'

'I assure you, I take my duties quite as seriously as the world's other presidents.'

'Good! We're so short you can umpire.'

'But I don't know the rules!'

He dismissed the objection. 'The charm of cricket is in the rules being simply an extension of civilized behaviour.' I handed him the cheque. 'I say! Thank you, Richard! We were only expecting about half that. While you've got your chequebook out, perhaps you'd write one for the tie? Price on the ticket, sorry it's rather stiff, but they're hand-made to order.'

First thing next morning, I found the greenhouse thicker with tomatoes than the Chinese New Year with scarlet lanterns. I brought a plastic sack of them into the kitchen, where Sandra was preparing our breakfast of tomato sausages and devilled tomatoes.

'For chrissake! What am I supposed to do with these?' she inquired.

'Tomato sauce?' I suggested uneasily. 'Much more wholesome than that slimy stuff in bottles. I know it sounds stupid, but I don't seem able to pick fast enough to catch up with them.'

She said faintly, 'I seem to remember an old Mrs Beeton recipe for tomato marmalade.'

'I expect it's jolly exciting on hot buttered toast.'

On my way home from surgery for lunch, I stopped in the High Street for a copy of Wisden's *Cricketers' Almanack*. I was horrified to find that the game had not rules but laws, all as unintelligible to me as the complex laws of genetics which professors write about in the *BMJ*. I turned the twenty-two closely printed pages of them while eating my tomato soufflé. I had discovered that the bat must not exceed $4^1/2$ inches in its widest part and be not more than 38 inches in length when the telephone rang. It was Bill Ightam.

I uttered to the consultant surgeon the same vague, jocular, hopeful remarks about Jilly making satisfactory progress as I had made, with bottled-up fear and fondness, to pedagogues since her finger painting and water play in nursery school.

'Quite one of the best registrars I've ever had.' Bill Ightam was short, dapper, amiable, blessed with the appellation on every lip of 'a very decent chap'. Also, I sent him private patients. 'I bet she gets her Fellowship first shot. Er, Richard. Er, you know my youngest daughter, Thomasina?' He added in a rush, 'Do you think she could play in the match tomorrow?'

I made a slight procrastinating noise deep in the larynx. Doubtless the Archbishop of Canterbury does the same when pressed about the ordination of women.

'As you know,' Bill Ightam continued, 'I have three other daughters, Edwina, Roberta and Georgina, but alas! No son.' He gulped. 'As I might one day hope to see play at Lord's. But Thomasina's a remarkable athlete, and dead keen on cricket. She captained the side at school – naturally, I sent her to the right one – and would absolutely adore turning out for Churchford. Oh, I know women's lib hasn't made a big stand at the wicket, they seem only concerned with uninteresting things like lesbianism. I put it to Windrush, and he said it was for the new president to decide.'

'My dear chap, as far as *I'm* concerned, Churchford can field the entire chorus line from the Palladium.'

'Thank you,' he said chokingly. 'Thank you…thank you…'

I swear I heard a sob as he rang off.

I avoided the greenhouse until that evening after dinner (cold tomato mousse). I was instantly gripped with terror. The structure was in danger of exploding and contaminating the district with tomato fallout. I filled a wheelbarrow and trundled it to the back door.

'Perhaps we could crush them in the bath,' I suggested weakly, as Sandra stared in speechless horror. 'Then buy a crate of vodka and invite our friends to the biggest Bloody Mary in Churchford.'

She muttered something about, God, why did I marry the world's only case of tomato alcoholism? I pushed the barrow to the vicarage. The vicar slammed the door, mentioning that Harvest Festival was not a moveable feast. I supposed his back was annoying him. I had the bright idea of telephoning Mrs Windrush and suggesting tomato sandwiches for tomorrow's game's tea interval, but they already had tomatoes as Job boils. I left them in the garage and hoped for vandals. I dreamed of tomato tendrils creeping upstairs like triffids.

The day of the match dawned grey. I brought Sandra the first trug of aubergines.

'It's moussaka time!' She gave a high-pitched laugh. 'Or maybe ratatouille with everything? Or aubergines *au gratin à la catalane, portugaise, toulousaine, grec* and *Imam Baldi*, which is fried with onions and currants, and in Turkish means the fainting priest because it smells so overpoweringly delicious, did you know? Did you know?'

She burst into tears. I did not mention the greenhouse containing enough ripe cucumbers to make sandwiches for every repertory production of *The Importance of Being Ernest* since Oscar Wilde got out of Reading Gaol.

The game started at noon. I was glad to leave home at eleven. Sandra was still sniffing, while filling jars of tomato chow-chow.

The Churchford cricket ground was delightful. A row of oaks occupied one side with the unassuming dignity of senior members in the pavilion at Lord's, the other was shielded by a lofty palisade of poplars. The ripe, unblemished green sloped gently to a spacious white-verandahed pavilion, in which I was pleased to notice white-clothed trestle tables with wives busy among cold chicken and strawberries, and equally so to spot on the bar a firkin of Huntsman's Double Hop, unadulterated since it moistened the jocular lips of Mr Jorrocks.

Pistol-shot cracks behind the pavilion led me to sinewy Windrush in flannels, practising against a young man's bowling in the nets with the dedicated air of having been at it since dawn.

'There's been a big development,' he said at once, sticking his bat under his arm and striding from the stumps.

14

'Do you know who's captain of Beagle Hill?' Windrush demanded. 'Mr Horace Fenny-Cooper! QC! The bastard!'

The name stirred the uneasiness of Big Brother's. 'The barrister who makes a killing bullying doctors in malpractice suits?'

Windrush nodded fiercely. 'Who specializes in extorting grossly inflated damages for minor errors. Why, the patients don't know how lucky they are! Lose the wrong finger or toe, take a world cruise and retire for life. Tax free, too, just like winning the pools. Hand in glove with the judges, of course. They all have a neurotic distrust of doctors.'

'Because they seldom send us to gaol, but we can always tell them to take their clothes off.'

'*They* make so many mistakes, they keep a special court sitting to correct them. Supposing they'd taken up medicine? My God! We'd have a housing problem with post-mortem rooms.'

I do not think I really like lawyers. Perhaps because they are trained to be nasty to people and we are trained to be nice to people. And doctors are spared from growing pompous. We have to look up too many fundamental orifices.

'Now's our chance to get our own back,' said Windrush warmly.

'That's up to your team.'

'It's up to you.'

'But I'm the umpire!'

'Exactly.'

I objected indignantly, '*That's* not in the spirit of the game.'

'Look, we've no more hope of beating Beagle Hill than Dr Barnardo's of winning the Cup Final,' he imparted frankly. 'Our team's half doctors, and I hear he's bringing a flock of lawyers, so this is a professional needle-match. Do you want the legal leech bragging round the Law Courts on Monday morning how he's pulverized us? Furthermore—' He eyed me sternly. 'Bill Ightam has a case pending. Stomach that went wrong.'

I said unhappily, 'I see a conflict of loyalties.'

'I don't.' Windrush returned to the nets.

I was left in the moral turmoil of E M (*Passage to India*) Forster, who speculated on having to choose between betraying his country or betraying his friend. I recalled that he hoped he would have the guts to betray his country, but perhaps he was just being clever. I decided on blunting the horns of the dilemma with a pint of Huntsman's Double Hop, but Bill Ightam's Rover appeared.

He proudly introduced Thomasina. She was quiet, slight, pink, eighteen, with an Adidas bag and two cricket bats, wearing jeans and a Sussex University sweatshirt. She was finishing her first year (artistic studies).

'I was desperately hoping to see her bat,' Bill said dotingly. 'But you know how it is – half a dozen private cases this afternoon, and Jilly's just phoned about a nasty abdomen.' He sighed. 'How I envy you! I'd still be umpiring, but I kept getting bleeped at the wicket.'

I became aware of a slight noise beside me. It was Windrush grinding his teeth. A latest-model Rolls-Royce was approaching down the track from the main road.

'That's him,' Windrush muttered pugnaciously, as Bill Ightam drove off. 'Look at that new Roller! Bought at we poor doctors' expense.'

Mr Horace Fenny-Cooper QC was six feet tall with shoulders like kerbstones, long thick black hair and a massive blue chin. Put in an identity parade, he would not stand a chance. He wore a bright-buttoned double-breasted blue blazer, with the gold and scarlet MCC tie. He advanced extending a large hand, assessing us under eyebrows like gorse bushes. I expected him to greet us with, 'Fe fi fo fum,' but he mentioned amiably, 'I hope the rain will keep off,' in the deep voice which could wring from a juryman's heart hundreds of thousands of pounds of other people's money.

Windrush uttered some saw about the swallows being high.

'Then we shall enjoy a grand game.' Mr Horace Fenny-Cooper QC gave a grin, as the Carpenter to the Oysters. 'If I always step to the wicket with the same feelings as I enter the court room – to wit, annihilating the opposition – is not this the great glory of our Constitution? Our law, like our games, like our politics, is surely confrontation between two sides, fought unsparingly, but observing manifest rules – some, I submit, unwritten – evolved over the centuries of our magnificent history?'

I suggested a pint of Huntsman's Double Hop, but he never drank before play.

'Dr Windrush – I put it to you, what is your speciality?'

'I'm a pathologist. All my patients have to be dead first.'

Mr Horace Fenny-Cooper QC grinned again. 'I am sure that spares you much trouble in litigation. You deal, if I may make the point, with the *fait accompli*. But whatever the verdict returned today –' His arm scythed the pleasant green view. 'I submit, every right-thinking man will, beyond reasonable doubt, remember that when the One Great Scorer comes to write against your name, he marks not that you won or lost but how you played the game. Shall we toss for innings?'

Windrush produced a coin.

'May I object? We have not yet exchanged lists of teams, which may not thereafter be changed. Law 1.'

Windrush took a scrap of paper from his flannels. He flicked. Mr Horace Fenny-Cooper QC won.

'We shall bat,' he pronounced, as if opening an agreeably sound case.

Windrush gripped my arm as the QC was extracting bats and pads from the boot of his Rolls.

'That little car bouncing by the pitch. It's Bill Ightam's houseman from the General. On call this weekend, up to his neck in patients, but Bill's given him the afternoon off. What terrific sportsmanship!'

I asked why.

'He's a Cambridge cricket blue,' he hissed.

'But he can't play.'

Windrush stared. 'Why ever not?'

'He's not in the team list you gave the opposing captain.'

'Don't be so petty. I'm sure the chap won't mind assuming the *nom de guerre* of someone who is. Only about half the side ever turn up.'

The teams trickled into their dressing rooms. Thomasina in white culottes and long white socks was cracking away hearteningly in the nets. I found a white coat, stamped PROPERTY OF CHURCHFORD GENERAL HOSPITAL. My fellow-umpire was a short, mild, bird-faced man, the most sought-after solicitor in Lincoln's Inn. I gathered ball, two bails and six coins. I was startled on stepping from the pavilion to encounter my son Andy, whom I had not seen for two months while he did cardiac research at St Swithin's, holding hands with a slim blonde in a black and red dress whom I had never seen at all.

'Dad!' he exclaimed. 'Mum said you were here. Meet Imogen. We're engaged.'

'Thank God! Andy!' Windrush appeared from the pavilion, distraught. 'We're one short. Find yourself a pair of flannels and field in the covers, will you?'

Andy disappeared. Windrush was already leading his team on the field. I paced with the birdlike solicitor to the wicket, my mind a kaleidoscope of my forthcoming daughter-in-law's possible qualities. I always treated our two children's followers with respect. However awful, they stood the chance of entering a companionship to be broken only with their attendance at my funeral.

The Beagle Hill innings was opened by Mr Horace Fenny-Cooper QC. His partner was a small, fat, tax barrister with large, round glasses. I stationed myself at square leg, inspecting Mr Horace Fenny-Cooper QC's generous gluteal region. The solicitor crisply called, 'Play.'

Our demon bowler, a Mayfair advertising executive, began to run. Mr Horace Fenny-Cooper QC raised a well-gloved restraining hand.

'Second slip,' he observed to me, 'is female.'

'No law against it.'

'Though it is, I submit, indubitably an irregularity in procedure.' He gave his smile. 'But I shall enter *nolle prosequi*.'

He rattled a defiant tattoo with his bat on the crease.

The first ball passed ten feet over his head.

The umpire signalled a wide.

The next struck the pitch just beyond the bowler's crease.

The umpire signalled a no-ball.

The third was another no-ball which whizzed past the QC's umbilicus, was grabbed by first slip, excitedly hurled at the wicket for a run-out and sped to the pavilion for four overthrows. Beagle Hill had six on the board, and the match had not yet begun.

The following ball crashed against the QC's pads.

'Howzat?' shouted all the fielders, and myself.

'Not out,' ruled the umpire stonily.

This dialogue was repeated five times, until he called, 'Over.' I reflected that barristers got their clients only from solicitors, as consultants their patients only from GPs, instilling among both professions a mutual interest in covering up each other's mistakes.

Windrush's young laboratory technician bowled neat medium-pace, which the little fat barrister hit briskly enough to keep on his feet the man who, pint in hand, hung metal numbers on the scoreboard. The spectators were depressingly outnumbered by the players. Andy's fiancée sat in a deckchair, wearing a wide black and red straw hat. She seemed to have nice legs. When I approached Andy for a word of fatherly congratulation, Windrush angrily waved at me for interfering with the fielders' concentration.

After three overs, our demon bowler, red-faced and damp-browed, was complaining of exhaustion.

'Can't risk the chap copping a coronary,' Windrush said humanely, letting him leave the field. 'I want to bowl him a lot, later in the innings. All right to lend us a sub?' he shouted to Mr Horace Fenny-Cooper QC, who inclined his head graciously.

A bright-faced Beagle Hill youngster sprang from the pavilion and eagerly took position inside the boundary rope. Tradition as old as the Men of Hambledon now ordained the field as keenly as any man of Churchford. Mr Horace Fenny-Cooper QC lofted the lab technician in the newcomer's direction.

'Catch it!' shouted all the fielders, and myself.

The substitute dropped it.

Mr Horace Fenny-Cooper QC lifted the next ball in the same direction.

The substitute dropped it again.

This was repeated four times.

It struck a glint in Windrush's eye, as a spark from flint. He started bowling his leg-spinners, delivered with an action resembling a pussyfooting octopus. This so confused Mr Horace Fenny-Cooper QC, he responded to the second one by hitting his own wicket.

'My goog!' Windrush confided exuberantly. 'On a good day I'd get through the entire West Indian batting order.'

Next batsman was Mr Horace Fenny-Cooper QC's usual junior, who specialized in instruments left inside. Two googlies later, I was surprised to notice the dismissed, still-padded QC re-enter the field.

'With respect, m'umpire,' he addressed me. 'The player who has just left the ground on urgent medical grounds is now downing a gin and tonic and smoking a cigar. I submit this is contrary to Law 2, also Law 46 (Duties of Umpires) Note 4(i).'

'Objection sustained,' said Windrush readily. 'Only thing to stop that little bugger dropping more catches, short of making him field behind an oak.'

Two more balls, and Windrush jubilantly bowled the new batsman for a duck. Mr Horace Fenny-Cooper QC again advanced from the pavilion.

'With great respect, m'umpire. My learned friend wasn't ready.'

'To me, he looked as ready as a virgin on her wedding night.'

'He wasn't ready in accordance with Law 25 Note 2(i).'

I said curtly, 'You're obstructing the field. Law 40. If you don't clear off, I'll give the other batsman out as well.'

He bowed. 'As your umpireship pleases.'

After another over I felt hungry and announced the lunch interval.

15

'Dad! Meet Imogen.'

Andy approached excitedly, sweater looped round neck, hand in hand with his fiancée at the pavilion steps.

But Mr Horace Fenny-Cooper QC had appeared at my elbow as disquietingly as a writ.

I remarked politely, 'May I introduce my son?'

Mr Horace Fenny-Cooper QC frowned. 'Indeed? But he appears on the nominated batting order – with which I was furnished by his captain before tossing for innings as Corncroft, T J.'

'I changed my name,' said Andy quickly.

'In*deed*?' The QC regarded him as he might a witness explaining that the bullion had dropped off the back of a lorry. 'It is undeniable, and I would not contest the fact, that Mr Corncroft bears a strong resemblance to yourself, Dr Gordon.'

'I changed it at the death-bed wish of a rich uncle,' Andy elaborated. 'In Canada. Keen to perpetuate the family name. Touching, don't you think?'

'So your wife's maiden name was Corncroft?' the QC said to me.

'No, it was Sandiford,' I replied automatically.

His eyebrows rose like gorse bushes in a high wind. 'Are you fencing with me?'

'Corncroft was my mother's mother's maiden name,' Andy told him. 'Naturally.'

'I put it to you,' he continued the cross-examination, 'the label on your sweater says R N Duckins.'

'Oh, that! I grabbed what gear I could. You see, I only joined the side when we were taking the field.'

'So! You were never in the official list? You confess?'

Andy snapped the fingers unattached to his future bride. 'I must have been! I phoned my sister last night at the General, and said to tell her houseman I'd be free to play. Ask him yourself,' he nodded in confirmation towards the Cambridge blue. 'Charley Barnes.'

'But *that* is Wilberforth, R N D.'

'So it is!' exclaimed Andy. 'They look very much alike.'

'Doubtless, brothers who have changed the names?' asked the QC with measured menace.

'Quite likely,' I agreed. 'There was dreadful incest in the family.'

'Might I remind you that you are on oath?'

'I'm not on anything, except tenterhooks that the Huntsman's Double Hop's running out.'

Mr Horace Fenny-Cooper QC slowly smiled. 'I beg your umpireship's indulgence. I rest my case. I was carried away. Often happens with you doctors, eh? Cut off more than you intended? Eh? Eh?'

He slapped my back and roared with laughter, sounding like the Marquis de Sade thinking up a fruity one.

'Dad, we've got to rush,' apologized Andy. 'We promised Mum we'd snatch a bite of lunch at home. She's making some fabulous tomato and aubergine pie. See you.'

They disappeared. I wondered what Imogen did for a living.

Returning after lunch, Andy leaped from his car, was put on to bowl and had the tax lawyer caught deftly by Thomasina. Replacing him came a wiry, flashing-eyed, briskly moustached Pakistani law student, whom we had been watching all morning with misgivings. He hit his first three balls for four, then swished so vigorously for six that his elaborate necklace broke, flew at the wicket and removed a bail.

'Howzat?' shouted all the fielders, and myself.

'Out,' I said.

While batsman and wicketkeeper gathered beads from the pitch, Mr Horace Fenny-Cooper QC reappeared.

'With utmost respect, m'umpire, that judgement was wrong in law.'

'The wicket is down if the striker's person removes either bail from the top of the stumps,' I stonewalled. 'Law 31.'

He gave an indulgent smile. 'With deepest respect, though the term "person" under Law 31 Note 5 includes the player's dress as defined in Law 25 Note 4, viz. the equipment and clothing of players as normally worn, I submit with all submission that this is not dress, to wit, decent covering, but ornament, i.e. decorative.'

'Not on your Nelly,' I said.

'I understand you are not conceding having acted *ultra vires*? Then I thank your umpireship.'

Windrush suddenly realized he had forgotten the Cambridge blue. He had him bowl and the opposition were all out in fifteen minutes for 110.

Between innings, I looked for Imogen.

'She went to the loo, and I expect got lost,' Andy explained. 'Excuse me, Dad – must pad up, I'm opening with Dr Windrush.'

Was Imogen middle-class? Working-class? Aristocracy? I wondered. Protestant? Catholic? Australian?

Mr Horace Fenny-Cooper QC opened the Beagle Hill bowling. Windrush was hit on the elbow, chin, ribs, toe, ear and scrotum, then retired hurt. He was replaced by Bill Ightam's houseman, who made 50 in three overs. He missed an off-break from the Pakistani student, which lodged in the pad top of the wicketkeeper – the substitute who had dropped the catches.

'How is that?' demanded Mr Horace Fenny-Cooper QC. 'Case of batsman caught by wicketkeeper's pads. Law 35 Note 4.'

'Not guilty.'

'Be a pal and pick it out,' the wicketkeeper invited the batsman. 'What with these gloves...thanks.'

'How is that?' repeated Mr Horace Fenny-Cooper QC, more loudly.

'Whoever heard of a batsman catching himself?'

'I am pleading under Handled the Ball, Law 36. He is *in flagrante delicto*.'

But Bill Ightam's houseman had tucked his bat under his arm and said he was going to retire anyway, to make a game of it. Thomasina was quickly bowled, followed at the wicket by Andy. During the next over, it drizzled. To needle Mr Horace Fenny-Cooper QC, I said as we reached the pavilion, 'You should have appealed for your last ball to T J Corncroft. I'd have given him out, plumb lbw.'

We decided to take tea. I searched for Andy and Imogen, but they were enjoying the intimacy of his car. What sort of accent had she? Kelvinside, Kensington or Kennington? I finished my Dundee cake. Play resumed. 'How is that?' Mr Horace Fenny-Cooper QC bellowed at once.

'But you haven't bowled yet,' I objected.

'I refer to the last ball. The appeal is permissible, because the next one has not been bowled nor has Time been called, as defined in Law 18. I cite Law 47. There is no stipulation of the time between balls. You've got to give him out. No case to answer.'

Andy left the wicket with the hurt and puzzled look of Esau arriving too late with the venison for his father.

Our last batsman arrived with our score only 80. The next over, he politely tapped an immobilized off-break back to the Pakistani student. Mr Horace Fenny-Cooper QC appealed for Hit the Ball Twice, Law 37. The following delivery, his bat and the wicketkeeper's knee shattered the wicket simultaneously.

'How is that?' called Mr Horace Fenny-Cooper QC feelingly. 'Hit wicket. Law 38 Note 1.'

'The batsman is Not Out if he breaks his wicket in avoiding being stumped,' I quoted. 'Note 3.'

'I must protest.'

'Don't argue. Law 46 Note 4(ii).'

Reckless in the justice of his cause, Mr Horace Fenny-Cooper QC appealed to his fielders, so passionately that in the confusion Churchford reached 100 with twelve overthrows before the polite batsman was run out.

'We've won!' exalted Mr Horace Fenny-Cooper QC.

'You haven't,' I said.

I pointed to the pavilion. Windrush was hobbling out in a motorbike crash helmet. Behind him walked Thomasina with bat and pads, to run between the wickets for the disabled batsman's shots.

'I'm resuming my innings,' he shouted to Mr Horace Fenny-Cooper QC. 'Law 33.'

The pavilion clock was eyed nervously by all the fielders, and myself. Eleven runs to win. Only an over to go.

'I've just discovered that Thomasina is the Sussex University 100 metres champion,' Windrush muttered in my ear at the crease. 'Watch her whizz between the wickets.'

'The runner,' complained Mr Horace Fenny-Cooper QC, approaching in outrage, 'must be dressed exactly like the batsman. Yours is wearing spiked running shoes.'

'OK, Portia, have your pound of flesh,' Windrush snarled at him. 'She can wear her sister's moped helmet, my spare flannels held up with the other end of this NHS bandage, and an Elastoplast dressing where you bloody near fractured my ulna.'

Play resumed. Windrush hit two, then three. Thomasina flickered to and fro like Francis Thompson's run-stealing Hornby and Barlow long ago. Windrush sneaked a single. Four runs behind! Three balls to go! A breathless hush. Broken by Mr Horace Fenny-Cooper QC roaring, 'Further objection! I beg to submit, the runner is *not* dressed as the batsman.'

'She looks lovely to me,' I said, as Thomasina stood panting at the stumps.

'Ha ha!' cried Mr Horace Fenny-Cooper QC, with the air of producing the missing murder weapon from under his wig. '*Is she wearing a box?*'

Thomasina hit him over the head with her bat.

It was instantly clear that the fielders needed to be treated as hostile witnesses. The prostrate Mr Horace Fenny-Cooper QC was borne from the wicket threatening litigation, if not prosecution – for assault, probably grievous bodily harm, possibly murder. As we all reached the pavilion, I said, 'I declare the match a draw.'

The casualty leaped to his feet. 'Of course it isn't a draw,' he said belligerently. 'We've three balls left. The way you were playing, we'd collar your last wicket.'

I retorted calmly, 'If the players have occasion to leave the field during the last over of the match, there shall be no resumption of play and the match shall be at an end. Law 18 Note 1.'

Mr Horace Fenny-Cooper QC glared. The muscles round his jaw, so powerful they could tatter doctors' reputations like masticating a tenderloin steak, twitched in frustration. 'I enter *nonsuit*,' he conceded curtly. 'But of course, with cricket it is not the result that counts. It is the spirit in which the game is played.'

He vanished into the dressing room, as abruptly as an unsuccessful criminal downstairs at the Old Bailey.

'That stupid law monger,' Windrush said gleefully. 'He hadn't the sense to spot that I wasn't wearing a bra. Thomasina, my dear! I award you your Churchford Cricket Club cap. I've a feeling that your father will be pleased. Come on, Richard, let's get stuck into the Huntsman's Double Hop.'

'I was looking for Andy and my potential daughter-in-law,' I protested.

'Oh, they had to rush back to London. Important research project, couldn't be left.'

I wondered if I should have liked her, had I ever got to know her.

16

I had a fortnight's annual leave left. Sandra wanted to go to the Côte d'Azur. I wanted to go fishing.

'*You're* the one who must toil for our living, my contribution to society is simply arranging the patients' flowers, so *of course* I'll go wherever you wish, darling,' she said.

Her tone was of Joan of Arc asking if they wanted a match.

Midsummer maddeningly revives the crammed waiting rooms of bleak bronchitic midwinter. The practice provisions itself with prescriptions for its holidays, or seeks safeguards against such renowned perils abroad as diarrhoea, typhoid, malaria, rabies and pregnancy. During a busy evening surgery, Mr Oldfield of the Gas Board sat down and silently stared at me.

'What's the trouble?' I asked briskly.

'It's not my trouble, doctor.'

'Then whose?'

He gazed into the corner beyond my left shoulder. 'Our son Roger. He's ten.'

'Well? What?'

He gazed into the corner beyond my right shoulder.

The Chestertonian grocer, apron peak buttoned on chest, rubbing his hands and inquiring, 'What's the next article?' from ladies seated on bentwood cane-bottomed chairs amid hempen cornucopias of sugar, salt, rice and split peas, lies extinct under a stratum of supermarkets.

The Wellsian draper, with pretty jumble of haberdashery, deep secretive drawers of combinations and bloomers, cash in little wooden pots whizzing across the ceiling like driven grouse, has been ploughed into the broad acres of chain-store counters.

The Dickensian pawnbroker's brass balls enjoy *in memoriam* the credit card.

The ruthless growth of population – and its wages – has dehumanized the petty transactions of everyday life.

The GP's surgery is likewise accused of becoming as impersonal as a cashpoint.

The A J Cronin doctor had time to chat, but fewer patients and even fewer remedies. I can cure with chemicals. I am far more valuable to my patients healing them with a scribbled prescription, than sitting impotently holding their hands and discussing the peculiarities of their relatives.

But those like Mr Oldfield demand duteous forbearance, to seek some truth unspoken through fear, embarrassment or ignorance.

I prompted, 'Fits? Nits? Squits? Be frank,' I urged. 'We doctors have heard it all before.'

'It's Swiss Army penknives.'

'Ah.'

'Roger's mad keen for one.'

'Nothing wrong with that. Wish I had one myself. Full of useful gadgets for taking stones out of chamois' hooves.'

'But I am concerned he wants to cut my whatsits off. What you doctors call the reproductive genitalia.'

I inquired, 'On what grounds do you suspect your little one will creep up on you – possibly when you are trimming your toenails after a bath, or perhaps bending to lift spuds in the garden, or simply leaning to adjust your set – and convert you into an instant countertenor?'

'I read it in a book.'

'Which book?' I asked shortly.

He drew a long breath. 'Though I am in charge of the gas meters of the entire county, I have enjoyed little of further education. It was straight from school to gas-fitting. Gas has been my life. Thus I am always trying to improve myself, doctor. I send for books – trial order, free approval, if not completely satisfied I will return the magnificent volume within ten days and will owe nothing, plus free gifts. After Christmas I learned the World of Art. Now I am into psychology.'

He fidgeted with his Gas Board tie. He was neat, with big gold-rimmed glasses, fair, balding and shy.

'This Freud, doctor, he says all sons are itching to do it on their fathers, then go and, you know, be naughty with Mum. It's a complex, isn't it?'

'Look –' I clasped my bald head in my hands. 'This is all in the mind. Obviously, it doesn't actually happen in families.'

'How do we know, doctor?' he asked darkly.

'Well, it does rather strike me as the sort of story which might get into the newspapers.'

'Then if it never happens, why did Freud think it all up?'

'Good question. Its symbolism. Imagery. If someone tells his girlfriend, You look so delicious I could eat you, he doesn't really mean he'd like her fricasseed with chips. If in a moment of irritation with a bus conductor you tell him to stuff his bus, you are not suggesting an interesting anatomical demonstration.'

He objected, 'It happened to this Oedipus.'

I mused, 'Oedipus! Son of the King of Thebes, who left him on a mountain with a spike through his feet. A fatal case of neonatal hypothermia, but for some passing shepherds. When he grew up, he unknowingly killed Dad after a row about right of way at a crossroads – odd, isn't it, they were as quarrelsome in traffic even then? He disinfested the neighbourhood of a monster which was making a frightful nuisance of itself, so they gave him the kingdom and the king's widow as bride. Who was of course Mother. The oracles had been speaking about little else for years. When the couple found out the truth they were so upset she hanged herself and he gouged his eyes out. It was a drama by Sophocles, but Noël Coward would have written it as a rather trying social predicament.'

Mr Oldfield persisted, 'If it's only a play like *The Mousetrap*, why does Freud so go on about it?'

'Another good question. The infant first loves his dear old mum – the titties, you know. Dad materializes later. Instant rivalry. The lad feels guilty. The Oedipus complex is Freud's basic family situation, though I fancy the worst that came of it is men marrying women like their mothers.'

I stopped. The classical had distracted me from the clinical. 'Buy young Roger a Swiss Army knife by all means,' I advised, ushering him out. 'He will doubtless use it for some perfectly wholesome purpose, like carving up the furniture. I assure you there is absolutely no need to go about like the Man in the Iron Mask, testicularily speaking.'

The next patients were Mr and Mrs Cuthbertson. They sat down and silently stared at me.

'What's the trouble?' I asked briskly.

'It's not our trouble, doctor,' said Mr Cuthbertson.

'Then whose?'

'Our son Cuthbert. He's twelve.'

'Don't tell me! You're scared he's going to castrate you and get into bed with Mum.'

'Doctor!' they cried.

They were globular, well washed, well laundered, dressed with decent drabness. 'He's playing truant,' explained Mr Cuthbertson.

'Dreadfully sorry. I had in mind the Oedipus complex. There's a lot of it about this time of the year. Lot of truancy, too,' I consoled them. 'Who wants to sit in a stuffy room learning algebra with the buttercups out and the swallows aswoop? In which school is he so conspicuous by his absence?'

'Balmoral House.'

I was puzzled. Truancy – now tarted up as school refusal, the way the physical education supervisor is really the gym mistress – usually occurred in families where the grove of Academe was regarded as less relevant to daily life than the bus shelter. Balmoral House was the boys' equivalent of St Ursula's, where the randy Watsons sent their daughter so bubbling with girlish glee for hockey and the pill. The fees were as straws to the entrepreneurial Watsons' backs. Mr Cuthbertson was an unimportant official in the Churchford Borough Treasurer's Department. His back had a painfully short breaking point for straws.

The Cuthbertsons' lives were ruthlessly pared to the comfortless bone by the fiercest British social ambition. Cuthbert would float out of

Balmoral House and find himself among the middle classes as Moses among the bulrushes.

Their ungrateful pride and joy was delivered daily but regularly made his escape, despite the Colditz point of view permeating the authorities. I inquired how he occupied himself when AWOL. 'Vandalism? Glue-sniffing? Pushing buttons on panda crossings and grinning infuriatingly at the stopped traffic?'

'Oh, nothing like that, doctor.' Mrs Cuthbertson looked horrified again.

'He sits on public benches,' said Mr Cuthbertson.

'Reading,' added Mrs Cuthbertson.

I asked with curiosity, 'Could I see your alfresco bookworm?'

She opened the consulting-room door, called 'Cuthbert!' and produced a small, pale, tidy child.

'So you're bored with school?' I greeted him amiably.

He replied, 'Positive.'

'I'm often dreadfully bored with medicine. But we must stick to our allotted jobs or it will be the end of civilization as we know it, which will probably be more fun.'

He replied, 'Negative.'

I asked, 'Reading anything interesting at the moment?'

'Bertrand Russell's *Principles of Mathematics*. But only because I'm interested in his opinions on Frege's *Foundations of Arithmetic*.'

'We have a problem,' I said.

He said, 'Positive.'

An idea struck me, as vividly appropriate as Sir John Millais' about the boyhood of Raleigh.

'Why not buy one of these home computer things?' I suggested to the Cuthbertsons. 'It'll absorb all young Cuthbert's mathematical energy, like a punchball if he were the sporty sort. After all, they cost no more than the set of toy trains which I used to buy my own children. Perhaps Balmoral House might contribute?' I urged. 'Surely the headmaster must see that he nurtures a budding Euclid?'

Cuthbert snorted contemptuously. 'Old Wartnose doesn't know enough maths to perm his pools.'

The Cuthbertsons hesitated but agreed, I felt because they suspected that a household without a computer is now regarded by the middle class as the equivalent of one which keeps the coal in the bath.

I drove to the golf club reflecting on a neat display of pastoral medicine. I had resolved two startlingly different family problems. It is unbelievable the nonsensical situations that between four walls become as steamed up as scraps of stew in a pressure cooker.

Leaning against the bar was Ollie Scuttle, consultant psychiatrist at the General. Psychiatrists are as well known inside the profession as out of it to vary from tolerable weirdos to outright nutters, but Ollie was so totally unintellectual he could be taken for a surgeon. I recounted the case of Oldfield Rex.

Ollie groaned. He was a big, gingery, rough-skinned man in a shaggy suit. 'Freud has much to answer for. Do you realize, before he set up couch, sex was for men an activity as normal as ferreting, racing whippets or playing dominoes. For women, as everyday as doing the washing and pickling onions. What's it now? A horizontal religion.'

'Mind, Freud did for dreams what Walt Disney did for mice,' I suggested sportingly.

Ollie said witheringly, 'Dreams are only to stop the long night being so boring. Look how tetchy people get, having the telly on the blink for one evening.'

Ollie did not seem a Freud fan. I confessed, 'I certainly feel dreadfully guilty whenever I dream of anything sticking out – the garden rake, the contents of the toolbox, my prescribing ballpoint. According to Freud, they all represent my plonker.'

'Yes, and dream of anything caving in, from the Cheddar Gorge to doughnuts, and you've really got in mind the gynaecologist's meal ticket,' Ollie agreed sombrely. 'You know why Freud camps out on God's grave? Because however dishonest, immoral, perverted, overbearing, unloving, selfish, ungrateful and generally impossible we are, it's the effect of the subconscious. Freud's made it no more our own fault than catching a dose of flu.'

Sipping his gin and tonic, Ollie added magisterially, 'Some men destroy their reputations with a book. Others with a sentence. I quote Freud in

1909: "I dislike the faint mental obfuscation that even a slight drink induces." What right has such a sobersides to sit in the stalls and criticize the human comedy?'

'Why, Richard—' came a soft voice.

It was Dr Quaggy, with his friendly air of a vulture inquiring about the health of its prospective dinner.

'Not had your holiday yet?' he asked solicitously. 'Ah, the pains of being Churchford's favourite GP! You certainly look as though you deserve a really good break.'

'End of the month I'm off trout fishing at Llawrfaennenogstumdwy.' I clarified, 'It's in Wales.'

'How delightful. I often wish I'd taken it up. Such an ideal occupation for retirement.'

I informed him crisply, 'Mindless activity is enjoyable only as an alternative to work.'

'*Over*work, Richard,' he corrected me gently. 'All of us in Churchford admire the way you push yourself to the limits. Pity about Charlie.'

'Charlie who?' I asked sharply.

He looked surprised. 'Charlie Pexham. Didn't you hear?'

'President of the Medical Society?'

'A coronary. Yesterday. He's in intensive care. Another GP who never spared himself.' He patted my arm. 'I'm sure your holiday will do you the world of good. Take care.'

He left me with an uneasy sensation. Perhaps young Oedipus felt the same when he first had a word with the oracles?

'Dr Pexham's had a coronary. He's in ITU at the General,' I informed Sandra sombrely when I reached home.

'Oh, dear! But you're hardly acquainted with him.'

'Never send to know for whom the cardiac arrest bleep sounds,' I recited gloomily. 'It bleeps for *thee*.'

'You really should cut down on your fats.'

'If God had meant men to avoid cholesterol, he would never have given us strawberries and cream and hot buttered crumpets.'

'Right after our holiday, I'm going to dedicate myself to being your dietician.' It struck Sandra agreeably. 'I'll buy a book tomorrow which gives absolutely all the nasty things in food, like salt and calories.'

I sighed. 'Modern morality is a battle between self-indulgence and hypochondria. I expect John Donne could have made something of that. I'm ravenous.'

17

Mr Warburton, headmaster of Balmoral House, appeared at the following morning's surgery with a tiny lump on the end of his nose.

'A fatty tumour, no danger whatever,' I reassured him. 'What we doctors call a lipoma. People get them all over. You'd be surprised at some of the places.'

He sat rubbing the nose. He was a lean, untidy man of forty, with lank fair hair, bulging blue eyes and leather on the elbows of his jacket. He asked what to do about it.

'Nothing. It's hardly noticeable.'

'It is to the boys. You'd think it was a rhino horn. What about plastic surgery?'

I mentioned NHS waiting lists.

'I can't possibly afford one of those private clinics you see advertised in the *New Statesman*,' he explained resentfully. 'Unfortunately I don't run Balmoral House with the commercial acumen of Dotheboys Hall.' He hesitated. 'In confidence, doctor – it mustn't get round that appalling crowd which my boys suffer the misfortune of possessing as parents – I'd sell out tomorrow, if I could. I've even a buyer – a college friend with the sense to work for one of those soulless crammers in Kensington, which I believe is so efficient it could get Laurel and Hardy into Oxford and Cambridge. But he can't raise the cash, no more than I can for my nose.' He fondled it again. 'Perhaps I'm too sensitive to be a schoolmaster.'

'But surely you're also sensitive to the wonderful challenge of education? To teach the young idea how to shoot, and so on?' I suggested encouragingly.

RICHARD GORDON

The remark nettled him, as though he had caught me throwing paper darts during religious knowledge. 'Education! What is it? Broadening the outlook. Instilling taste, honesty. Forming character. Identifying truth and beauty. Offering a sense of values. And what do my parents want? Top-grade A-levels, so their children can collect jobs as business executives with full pension rights. What would you expect of people who fit their homes with natural-pine kitchens, holiday on Costas and have the ambition only to own a Mercedes? My job's the labours of Hercules with someone performing a time and motion study.'

I suggested, 'Like my private patients, who become demanding when paying for something others have to suffer for free.'

He became heated, waving his spindly arms. 'Compulsory education! Utterly outdated, since the days when children squeaked up two plus two on slates. Who needs the three Rs in a world of TV, word processors and calculators? They seem to get along pretty well without it in Hong Kong. Education should be an activity only for those with a powerful urge to do it, like rock climbing. Had I charge of the country's...the world's...education, I should create a select audience for the pageant of life, who could follow the plot without distraction by its gaudy and tawdry scenery. Can't you do anything at all about my wart?'

'Perhaps the boys will get bored with it?'

'No way.'

'Take their minds off it,' I suggested ingeniously. 'Develop some endearing eccentricity. Say, always having your zip undone.'

He was unimpressed.

At the door I mentioned, 'I believe you've a sprouting genius called Cuthbert Cuthbertson?'

He snorted. 'Awfully boring boy. Beastly little swot.' He had a final fiddle with his lump. 'I'll have to come to terms with it, I suppose. After all, Cyrano de Bergerac had the same problem.'

I have often found schoolteachers unbalanced. It is from the strain of always having to behave like adults.

Three patients later came Mrs Myrtle Oldfield. Unlike Oedipus, Mr Oldfield had married someone entirely different. She was a big, bubbly redhead, former salesperson at Robbins Modes, local arbiter of fashion.

114

'I really do not know what's got into my Harry about our Roger,' she began. 'Who I'm proud to say is a model child, and whom I have just left happily at the Beowulf Comprehensive.'

'Got his Swiss Army penknife yet?'

'Oo! So you know, do you? Honestly, Harry has such a thing about it, he says he will not place such an implement in innocent hands. Of course you read in the papers about youngsters slicing up old ladies and that, but the way Harry's creating you'd think Roger was going to murder his parents in their beds. It's getting on my nerves, doctor, something awful.'

'Harry's unnecessarily worried about the Oedipus complex.'

'What puss?'

I explained how all sons wished to castrate Father and marry Mother.

Mrs Oldfield laughed. 'I can see it now! Me in bridal white with orange blossom, standing at the altar with Roger, he'd just come up to my hips. Oh, it would be a lovely wedding. I suppose Roger would have to go easy on the champagne, but he just loves iced fruit cake. I wonder where we'd go for our honeymoon?' she speculated. 'Roger liked Littlehampton, but only because of the Peter Pan paddling pool, I don't suppose many newly married couples go for it, still it would be handy taking your hubby everywhere half-price, wouldn't it? And just think! Marrying your own little boy, you'd have no trouble with the in-laws. It's a lovely idea, doctor.'

I expressed the wish that my other patients were as robustly sensible, and assured her, 'The complex has no more effect on your everyday life than the stirrings of the earth's core on the foundations of your charming little bungalow.'

'Of course not, doctor. Well, you make me feel better already. I tell you what, I'm going to buy Roger one of those Swiss Army knives myself, even if Harry is terrified the little boy's going to use it to vandalize the family jewels. Harry does get some funny notions in his head, you'd be surprised, you should hear him going on about people staring in the street because of his pimples. Though I must say, if Roger's going to inherit *those* I'll turn his proposal down flat.'

Odd, it occurred to me. Mr Warburton shared a sensitivity about facial blemishes with Mr Oldfield. Did he suffer also a phobia of mass castration by the pupils of Balmoral House? I must ask Ollie Scuttle at the golf club.

The next day was Saturday. I paused on my way home from surgery to replenish my cellar with fine wines. In the supermarket, I met Mr Cuthbertson.

'Doctor!' he greeted me warmly. 'Wonderful idea of yours. About the home computer. Little Cuthbert is no longer a problem child. He's as happy as the day is long, toddling off to school then coming home to potter among the square roots and cosines. Furthermore –' He tugged from his jacket pocket a copy of the pink-paged *Financial Times*. 'He's using the computer to have a go at this.'

His finger indicated an advertisement by a firm of City stockbrokers. To hook reluctant capitalist debutants, they were offering a £1000 prize for picking the twenty shares likely to go up most on the London Stock Exchange over the month.

'Even I cannot understand these pages of share prices and dividends and that,' Mr Cuthbertson confessed proudly. 'And I am in control of the borough's total budget for recreational activities and toilets.'

I wished them luck. Another case cured. Our trolleys went their separate ways.

Mr Cuthbertson appeared at Tuesday evening surgery.

'Doctor, something terrible's happened.' He sat down, trembling. 'Young Cuthbert. Oh, the shame!'

'What's the matter? Lost the knack? Always a risk with infant prodigies. They were saying Mozart was washed up at six.'

'Cuthbert's been collared, doctor. By the school attendance officer.'

'Oh? What was he up to?'

'Sitting on a bench in the park, reading the *Investors' Chronicle*.'

The distraught father enlarged on the incident. The official seemed to have been a former member of the Special Patrol Group, or maybe the SAS, or possibly the Gestapo.

'To think! Me a council employee!' His voice broke under the crushing humiliation. 'Now I know how the Pope felt when those Vatican bankers got shopped for fiddling. Poor misunderstood Cuthbert! He'll be dragged through the juvenile court, you mark my words. Being no respecter of authority, particularly of our big-headed magistrates – and I could tell you a thing or two about their expense sheets – he could be sent to borstal; a sensitive lad like Cuthbert, it would kill him. What are we to do, doctor?'

'Send an SOS to Balmoral House,' I suggested.

'No, no,' he objected agitatedly. 'Not since the headmaster went so peculiar.' He dropped his voice. 'Mr Warburton seems to be performing what they call indecent exposure, all over the school. Even in prayers and assembly. The boys are all laughing themselves silly, they think it's the biggest joke since the science master blew his fingers off, but the parents are calling a special meeting.'

My affinity with Balmoral House suddenly expired, like young Cuthbert's.

'Mr Cuthbertson,' I pointed out, 'it is hardly your doctor's job to rub out the blots on your escutcheon. I have a roomful of patients outside who require me for my proper function of opening their bowels, syringing their ears, supporting their varicose veins, stiffening their resolve against impotence, and similar matters with profound effect on human happiness.'

'But doctor,' he implored, 'you're always so kind to humble, struggling people like us.'

I sighed. I had the uncomfortable feeling of a sensitive plant with greenfly. 'Very well, I'll have a word with the local education authority,' I promised. 'Perhaps young Cuthbert's scholastic attitudes will ripen with the apples. A hols is a long time in childhood, the summer one a lifetime.'

Mr Cuthbertson took my hand in both his. 'Thank you, doctor,' he said feebly. 'We can but be ever grateful to those who know so much more about the ways of the world. Bless you.'

I had the rewarding sensation of performing a useful stroke of pastoral medicine. However outlandish the forces bringing patient to doctor, however pressing the doctor's practice – or his pleasures, or his personal problems – the patient always comes first. The tradition was founded by Hippocrates two thousand years ago. Politicians are frequently mistaken in imagining they created the medical profession the same day as the NHS.

Late one afternoon at the end of the month, I left my car at Straker's garage for servicing before my fishing holidays. Mr Cuthbertson was gazing into the showroom window, smoking a cigar.

'Hello, doctor! I just looked in to order a Merc.'

'Oh?' I said.

'Have a Havana. Ah, you don't, of course. Had your holiday yet? We're just off to the South of France.'

'Oh?' I said.

'Know any good French restaurants, cafés, discos and that?'

It seemed that Uriah Heep had changed into the Man Who Broke the Bank at Monte Carlo. 'How's the young hopeful?' I inquired.

'We won! That share competition. Announced this morning. Look.' He flourished a pink cutting.

'Congratulations,' I said benevolently. 'You got the thousand-pound prize? Well, even these days, it's a tidy sum. Perhaps you're right to blow it on a glamorous holiday.'

He grinned. 'Listen, doctor. As befits a member of the Borough Treasurer's staff, I have always been prudent with money. But when my son and heir was pinched by the heavies, it altered my thinking. What point was there, living a respectable life when they can run you in for sitting in the sun reading about the International Monetary Fund? Also, I have a thousand times more faith in my little one than in his teachers. So I drew our nest egg from the building society and backed his hunches in the Stock Exchange competition. For real.'

Mr Cuthbertson flicked away his last four inches of cigar. 'Well, what with Megaglomerates International and Hyperinvestments Incorporated taking over each other, and that Boomerang Trust finding the entire Australian desert was floating on oil, little Cuthbert and me did pretty nicely, thank you. So I am giving up the borough toilets to set up with Cuthbert as a financial adviser.'

I whistled. 'What's old Wartnose think?'

He lit another cigar. 'Over the moon. He did a bit of wheeler-dealing with some sharp schoolmaster in London and took a job with OXED – this organization that goes out to teach kids in Africa geometry and Latin and that. So little Cuthbert is now joint owner of Balmoral House,' he ended proudly. 'Can hardly wait for prayers and assembly first day of term, though I think they've abolished prayers, the education being scientifically planned by computer so no longer needing the guidance of God.'

I said humbly, 'Might I express the respectful hope that little Cuthbert will remember me when he's a millionaire?'

But he did not even offer me a lift home.

Sandra was in the front garden of our Victorian villa, agitated.

'The Oldfields,' she shouted. 'Urgent call.'

I inquired about what.

'Couldn't make a word of sense. They're hysterical, the lot of them. You'd better take my car and hurry over.'

I found Mr Oldfield clutching the front gate between the holly encircling his charming little bungalow.

'Don't go in there, doctor,' he whimpered.

'Why?'

'It's Myrtle.'

'What's the matter with her?'

'She's trying to castrate me with a Swiss Army penknife.'

'That's not in Sophocles' plot,' I objected.

'This is Linda, doctor.'

A girl in anorak and jeans appeared round the hedge.

'Hello,' said Linda.

'I love her, doctor,' said Mr Oldfield.

'Oh?' I said.

'Linda is in Gas Board accounts (new connections),' he explained shakily. 'Doctor, I just thought up all that stuff about Freud. I was going to buy Roger the Swiss Army penknife when Linda had her holidays, then clear off because I was scared of him going for my personals. But what happens? Myrtle buys him one, so I say I'll be happy to leave her with Roger and forgo the operation, but Myrtle does not seem to take kindly to the idea. What shall I do?'

'My advice is to buy the works of Jung. He was a Swiss, and probably has a lot on the psychology of their Army penknives. Good evening.'

I am leaving pastoral medicine to the vicar of St Alphege's, who believes that Hell yawns for adultery, truancy and parking outside the churchyard, though, I fancy, only when his back is troubling him.

18

We arrived at Llawrfaennenogstumdwy as the sun stretched western mountain shadows across the river Abergynolwnfi, frothing its way excitedly among boulders before pausing to catch its breath in smooth, tree-canopied pools. I drove along the twisting riverbank road tingling with the prospect of hauling out trout like a piscine sausage machine.

'Now, I don't want you to fret about me at all this holiday,' Sandra implored. 'I only want you to relax and enjoy yourself.'

I said defensively, 'I know you'd prefer the Med, but honestly, I'm fed up with crowded airports, garlic and lunatic Alfa drivers. Anyway, bright sunlight has a worse effect on the skin than neat vodka on the stomach.'

'I was being utterly selfish, darling,' she continued contritely. 'I shan't be in the slightest bored, I shall sit on the bank and watch. I've brought lots of Agatha Christies and my tatting, and if it rains there's always television in Welsh, which must he interesting. It's *you* who needs to unwind and recharge your batteries after the stress of overwork, and if I *did* want to see Cannes, well, there's other years.'

'You sound like Dr Quaggy,' I grumbled.

A final twist revealed the Rising Trout Hotel, a turreted red-brick wysteria-decked mansion arising amid hydrangeas, with croquet lawn, putting green and gazebo.

'Looks all right,' Sandra admitted.

'Well, I heard about it from this Panacea Drugs salesman, and they do themselves sybaritically, travelling on expenses.'

A slight, sandy man in blue blazer, sharply creased grey trousers and striped tie hurried down the stone front steps.

'Mr Gordon? Colonel Coots. A pleasure, welcoming you to my hotel.'

'How's the fishing?' I demanded.

'Stupendous. Fantastic. Never known it better. Last week's guests were thinking of clubbing together for a Birdseye frozen-food lorry, to take their catch home. Sniffed our wonderful mountain air? Does miracles for tired businessmen. You're in life insurance, I believe?'

I nodded. I was also fed up on holiday with fellow-guests cadging medical advice, having fits or babies, or dropping dead, putting me to endless trouble.

'I'm sure you'll be very satisfied with the Cyhiraeth room – a Celtic goddess of the streams, you know. Bronwen! The bags!'

From the Gothic front door appeared a grinning teenage blonde in black skirt and thin white blouse. She was the most advanced case of mammary hyperplasia I had seen. They were like Belisha beacons.

'You'd be from London, would you?' Bronwen led us into a mullion-windowed room overlooking the river.

'Yes, I have an office there, insuring lives.' I stared, fascinated. They seemed about to burst from their bra like the start of a hot-air balloon race.

'It must be lovely, living in London and that, and going to all those discos.'

'We don't terribly often,' murmured Sandra.

'I'm sure you'll find the bed comfy. Brand-new mattress. Sponge rubber.' She bounced it vigorously.

'Very pneumatic,' I agreed.

'You'd like me to give you a cup of tea in bed?'

'Very much.'

'Dinner's roast chicken. If you want me any time, just ring.' I fumbled for money. 'Oooo! Thank you, sir.'

'You grossly overtipped that girl,' complained Sandra as the door shut.

'In a place like this it's essential to establish good relations with the staff. Bad service would utterly ruin my relaxing holiday.'

I swished in the lofty room my expensive new carbon rod, which the tackle-shop man assured me would catch fish in the Sahara. I inspected my costly aluminium reels, floating and sinking lines, and buffet of mouth-watering fishing flies. I had visited the shop for a couple of cheap nylon casts, but was carried away like Aladdin and ended with hand-warmer, boot-dryer, trout-smoker, pairs of thermal underwear, dozen salmon-decorated sherry glasses, set of hunting-scene tablemats, and ultrasonic Japanese device for scientifically repelling mosquitoes, which I later suspected of emitting the mating call of Welsh ones.

Leaving Sandra to unpack, I descended to a timbered bar decorated with the cased corpses of fish. Already into his gin and tonic was Sir Rollo Basingstoke, Surgeon to the Queen.

'Rollo, you old bastard!' He was a handsome thickset man with thick grey wavy hair and thick-framed glasses. 'Haven't seen you since that wine and cheese party.'

He grabbed my lapels. 'I am Mr Basingstoke, director of the Mayfair estate agents Basingstoke and Bolingbroke.' He hissed, glaring into my eyes, 'I heard of this hideaway from a Panacea Drugs rep, and I've already had enough holidays ruined by acute abdomens at two in the morning. Can't charge a fee, either. So keep your mouth shut, doctor.'

I objected, 'You've got the wrong chap. I'm Mr Gordon, a life insurance salesman. Ask the Colonel,' I mentioned, as he appeared behind the bar.

We guffawed loudly. 'Written any good policies lately?' Rollo inquired.

'Not bad. We're doing jolly well out of hang-gliding. How's the property racket?'

'Land's the one commodity they can't make any more of, you know.'

'What a brilliant thought!'

'Rollo!' exclaimed Sandra from the door.

'Ssssshhhhh!' He applied his lips to her ear.

She smiled. 'But how nice to enjoy Lady Basingstoke's company,' she whispered back, 'while our menfolk are catching our dinner.'

Sandra is impressed with her Ladyship. She does not know her as I did, a sexy staff nurse on orthopaedics who threw up over the sub-dean at a hospital party.

The dining room was dark-panelled, decorated with sporting prints, and staffed by Bronwen embellished with a little frilly apron.

She leaned over me solicitously. 'Breast or leg?'

'Breast.'

'But you *never* eat the white meat at home!' exclaimed Sandra.

'Holiday's time for a change,' I said uneasily.

The next day was lovely. I caught nothing.

The colonel shook his head knowingly. 'The water's too murky. The peat, you understand. Ruins it, bad as dregs in port. Wait till next week, you'll be beating off the rising fish with the butt end of your rod.'

Rollo caught nothing, either. I found him chatting over gin and tonics in the bar before dinner with a pleasant-looking fellow introduced as Dalrymple.

'I'm a chartered accountant,' Dalrymple conveyed at once. 'You're in life insurance? Must be a jolly harrowing job, I mean, wondering which customer will expire next and demand his money back.'

I agreed quickly. 'Give me Russian Roulette before breakfast any time. But you,' I diverted him, 'must be frightfully clever fiddling people's income tax?'

'Nothing to it,' he assured me airily. 'All done by computers, easy as playing Space Invaders in amusement arcades.'

I was outraged. 'My accountant claims he sweats blood over those bits about woodlands and housekeeper being a relative and payments under the Irish Church Acts.'

Dalrymple grinned. 'And charges for it? Got to preserve the mumbo-jumbo of the accountancy profession.'

Rollo laughed. 'Like the medical profession.'

I winked at him fiercely.

Rollo added hastily, 'Wasn't it Shaw who said all professions were conspiracies against laity?'

'Oh, doctors,' said Dalrymple disgustedly. 'Never tell you *anything*, do they? You should hear about my sister.'

'Please,' invited Rollo eagerly.

'She went to the doctor and said she'd this funny feeling up and down her spine. The doctor gave her some pills. They give pills for everything, don't they? Broken legs, I wouldn't be surprised. You won't believe it, but the very next week she came out all over with chicken-pox.'

I rubbed my chin. 'Sure it wasn't shingles? The two conditions are related, you know, same virus. Shingles often starts off with funny feelings in the skin.' Rollo violently elbowed me. 'My aunt had it during the war,' I explained. 'She has talked of little else since.'

We were joined by another decent-looking chap introducing himself as Harrington.

'I'm a commissioner for oaths,' he volunteered.

'Must be interesting,' I murmured politely.

He gave a low whistle. 'You'd be amazed at some of the oaths people commission these days. You're in the Cyhiraeth room? Did you know the shriek she used to utter foretold imminent death?'

'Like a crash bleep for the cardiac arrest trolley,' mentioned Dalrymple with a laugh. 'I mean, you're always seeing it on television.'

'I'm hooked on the medical programmes,' Harrington agreed. 'Those miraculous heart transplants! Mind, they don't seem to do the patients much good, but they're wonderful for the surgeons' exhibitionism.'

'The sight of blood makes me faint.' Rollo held a hand over his eyes.

'I've a distant cousin who's a surgeon,' Harrington amplified. 'Specializes in the feet. Never examined a patient above the ankle in his life.'

I asked about big property deals up Rollo's sleeve.

He dropped his voice. 'Yes! Top secret. I've been retained by Her Majesty to dispose of Windsor Castle to a consortium of Arabs. Unbelievable, isn't it?' The accountant and commissioner of oaths stared wide-eyed. 'It's for pressing reasons of State, which I certainly won't divulge. I've just sent out the particulars: period residence, easy reach London and airport, stone-built, extensive views and many interesting features. I was putting my name on a board outside the front gate, but the authorities are proving rather petty.'

Bronwen appeared behind the bar. We fell silent. We gazed upon the Delectable Mountains. 'Can I get you anything to drink, now?'

'Four gin and titties,' I said. 'Tonics,' I said.

'Large ones?'

'Enormous,' I said.

19

A week passed. I had caught nothing. Neither had Rollo. The colonel eyed the river penetratingly. He said the water was too clear.

I met in the bar an agreeable new arrival called Forshaw.

'What's your line of country?' he asked amiably. 'Snap! So am I. What insurance company?'

'The Rocksolid,' I replied hastily. I knew of it only because my life's savings were deposited therein.

He whistled. 'Lucky sod.'

'Really?' I asked vaguely.

'Their sales commission, of course. Know what we say in the trade?' He grinned. 'Rocksolid bribe their reps so much to flog policies, it's a wonder there's anything left in the kitty for the customers.'

I asked in alarm, 'I hope they're not going bust?'

He laughed. 'Well, they say your directors sleep with tickets to South America and dark glasses at the bedside. Tell me, how do you calculate your actuarial index?'

'Never talk shop on holiday,' I said severely.

I slunk out, saying I had just remembered that I never drank before meals, doctor's orders.

It rained for three days. I had still caught nothing. Neither had Rollo. The colonel declared thoughtfully that the water was too drumbly. I asked shortly what drumbly meant. He looked pained, and said he imagined that every real fisherman knew about drumbly.

Sandra said at dinner, 'Don't keep looking down Bronwen's cleavage like that when she serves the soup, people are beginning to nudge.'

I said, flustered, 'If Quasimodo was serving it, I wouldn't notice the hump?'

She persisted severely, 'I'd have imagined boobs as boringly commonplace to you as udders to farmers.'

I took a lofty artistic tone. 'The female breast is never drained of its Rubenesque beauty. As a sixteenth-century poet carolled, *Heigh ho, fair Rosaline! Her paps are centres of delight, Her breasts are orbs of heavenly frame.* Quite charming.'

'You're just a dirty old doctor,' Sandra corrected me.

Rollo, Dalrymple, Harrington and myself enjoyed a long talk in the bar after dinner about the effect of property values on life insurance, accountancy and oath commissioning, and vice versa. We were surprised when the colonel announced testily it was well past midnight and he was locking up. I tripped over a suitcase which Sandra had stupidly left in the middle of the bedroom floor. She expressed the hope from the pillow that next year I should be able to find an alcoholics' home with fishing rights.

In the morning Sandra stayed in the lounge with a book of crossword puzzles. She said that my catching nothing for ten days gave her the feeling of sitting to watch the trees grow, which was hardly less interesting, furthermore Lady Basingstoke seemed to imagine she was a combination of Princess Di and Mrs Thatcher, also she sensed a nasty cold coming on, but if the holiday was relaxing me she would not give all this a second thought.

I caught a fish! I hastened back to display it.

'*That?*' cried Sandra. 'Why, if it was in a tin of sardines, it would contravene the Trade Descriptions Act.'

I was deeply hurt. 'I shall lay it in state with the other catches on that marble slab in the hall,' I told her with dignity.

'Then I shall disown both of you.' She returned to her crossword. 'I've just turned said Pepys into dyspepsia.'

Rollo was laying a fish on the slab, too.

'Mine's bigger than yours,' I claimed at once.

'Of course it isn't,' he replied huffily.

'It is.'

'It is *not!*'

'A good quarter-inch in it. Look.'

'Rubbish. It's the way you're positioning them.'

'Are you accusing me of being unsporting?'

He drew himself up. 'I shall obtain a ruler.'

Measuring, he exclaimed triumphantly, 'There! A clear three-eighths of an inch in my favour. I should be obliged if in future you did not cast slurs on my veracity.'

I decided that surgeons fish in the same spirit as they practise, ruthlessly competitively. The colonel told me as I returned the ruler that the water was now too high. Tomorrow the fish would be leaping thicker than the midges.

Rollo was up to something. Next morning after breakfast he slipped off with a veal and ham pie and a bottle of claret. In Cyhiraeth, Bronwen was making the bed. She asked as she bent to her work about the availability of pop concerts in London and if I knew any of the stars. Lovely view.

On the front steps stood Mr and Mrs Forshaw, whom I had been avoiding by dodging behind trees and into the loo. After chatting about the weather, Mr Forshaw asked, 'What's your portfolio?'

'Samsonite,' I said.

He stared, then laughed. 'I like it! But what are you holding?'

I looked. 'A fishing rod.'

He slapped his thigh. 'We need a few comics in the business. Who's your broker?'

'I don't know, except he's got three balls.'

He did not laugh so heartily, and looked at me from the sides of his eyes. I strolled away noticing him muttering something to his wife and tapping his forehead.

I caught nothing. The colonel stared, assessing the water, and expertly pronounced it too flat. We thought of leaving for home early. Sandra had finished the crosswords.

As everyone sat down to dinner, the colonel appeared, agitated.

'Ladies and gentlemen,' he implored. 'Could you help yourselves from the kitchen hatch? Young Bronwen's been suddenly taken ill. I must phone for the doctor.'

I exclaimed, 'What's she got?'

He replied distractedly, 'I don't know, but it's something the matter with her chest.'

I instantly stood and pronounced, 'Don't worry! I am a doctor.'

So did Rollo, Dalrymple and Harrington.

I persuaded Sandra to stay.

On our last day, the colonel eyed the river, shook his head and declared that the water was too normal. I caught a huge fish.

'Well, it's Moby Dick compared to the other one,' Sandra conceded. 'It'll end your holiday usefully relaxed, even if it's the biggest miracle since the feeding of the five thousand.'

As I proudly lay it on the post-mortem slab, Rollo appeared puffing under the weight of two supermarket bags crammed with fish.

'Congratulations!' I exclaimed, green as the river weed with envy. 'What brilliance. What skill.'

'It's easy if you know how,' Rollo imparted modestly. 'Like surgery.'

'I suppose,' I advanced under the camouflage of a laugh, 'you weren't using one of those powerful hormonal baits? Or maybe a lump of gorgonzola?'

He lowered his voice. 'No, but I found from the local community medicine feller where the village sewer's been leaking into the river all summer. The fish are as thick there as customers in McDonald's on a Saturday night.'

'You might have told *me*,' I complained bitterly.

'I wanted to, after breakfast. But you'd disappeared to go over Bronwen's chest again. You can't have everything, can you? Will you and Sandra join us tonight, to help out with the eating? I happen to know that the colonel has an excellent bottle or two of Mersault '78.'

20

The season of mellow fruitfulness found Mrs Iles pregnant. I beamingly congratulated her.

'You're the one I've got to thank for my condition,' she asserted.

'Oh, come.' I pushed half-moons half down nose. 'My intervention in the process was brief, if satisfying.'

'Honestly, I'd like to run round telling everyone, "It's all the doctor's doing!" But I suppose it's best to keep quiet and let the neighbours think it's my husband's?'

I nodded gravely. 'I've put several ladies in your position, and I always suggest exactly that.'

She had been married ten years (husband in biscuits). She had tried everything. Relaxing Caribbean cruise. The kama sutra position. Oysters. Prayer. Catnip (recommended by Cromwellian herbalist Nicholas Culpepper). The couple desperately consulted me in early summer. I referred her to Bertie Taverill, gynaecologist at the General, who found her as fertile as the meadows of May. The microscope pointed accusingly to her husband.

Thelma Iles was gingery, gentle, freckled and floppy. Edgar Iles was small, spectacled, energetic and edgy. He needed strenuous explanation that a low sperm count was unrelated to masculinity, aggressiveness, vigour, sexiness or management skills, and afflicted 1500 lusty fellow-countrymen a year. He had built up his biscuit business from crumbs, and desperately desired bequeathing it to a devoted son, subject to capital transfer tax avoidance. I suggested AID.

'But what if the child comes out cross-eyed?' he objected nervously. 'Bowlegged? A nitwit?'

'Not to mention the er,' added Mrs Iles. 'You know, doctor. The ethnic bit.'

'The anonymous donors are screened far more carefully than the secret service,' I reassured them. 'Physically, mentally and er. Why, a couple of thousand Britons are conceived thuswise every year, to general satisfaction. A whole quarter of a million are already walking about the Western world, without attracting shudders.'

Mrs Iles hesitantly inquired about technical details. Simplicity itself, I extolled: the lady has a quick affair with a syringe and a little lie-down afterwards. The specimen could be fresh or frozen, like smoked salmon. They agreed to consult a discreet doctor in Wimpole Street recommended by my son Andy, who seemed to know about such things. Now sperm and ovum had met like Romeo and Juliet, and Mrs Iles sat across the consulting desk like the cat who had eaten the cream purring at the milkman.

'Though I cannot keep out of my mind the gentleman,' she confided coyly. 'I mean, was he handsome and distinguished like Prince Charles? Talented like Terry Wogan? Domineering like Robin Day? Or perhaps terrifically brainy? I keep reading how those Nobel prizewinners are offered as donors, just like Miss Worlds to open dairy shows.'

'The secret will never be known,' I told her cosily, 'being locked away in the doctor's files in Wimpole Street.'

'I suppose it'll be a little bastard?' she asked sadly.

'I'm afraid so. The law is less an ass than a mule, which combines stubbornness with sexual incompetence. But don't worry, without bastards we shouldn't have much of an English aristocracy.'

She thanked me profusely and left a tin of de luxe chockie bikkies.

I reflected how complicated ethical problems had grown since I was a young doctor, when the only one was presented by a panting half-naked wife alone in the house, and you had to face gravely the chances of getting away with it.

Sandra greeted me at lunchtime, 'Andy phoned from St Swithin's. He's home for a few days towards the end of the month.'

'Good! With Imogen?' She shrugged. 'I'd love to meet her. How was she, during that cricket match? Nice? Quiet? Sense of humour?'

'Oh, bubbling! In fits at Andy describing what a fool you were making of yourself as the umpire.'

I changed the subject. 'Perhaps Dr Quaggy's right. Should I retire? I know, my dear, how you yearn for the warming sun like a newly planted tulip bulb. Why not transform my life into an everlasting holiday? Why not enjoy our castle in Spain – on a time-share basis, of course? Why should I linger in a profession with the top rate of alcoholism, suicide and hypochondria? There may be no retiring age for GPs, but why should I lay a shaky stethoscope on patients who are either alarmed at the medical Methuselah or reassured that their doctor has stumbled upon the secret of eternal life?'

'You'd be bored,' Sandra informed me. 'Without patients, you'd be like Dr Barnardo without waifs.'

I tucked into my cholesterol-free saltless salad. Since adopting the hobby of dietetics, Sandra had become as lunatic about food as Dr Lonelyhearts' Scots professor of nutrition. 'I'd miss mitigating human miseries and joining in its joys,' I admitted. 'Today I'd a lady who'd found pregnancy as elusive as I found fish in Llawrfaennenogstumdwy.'

'With AID and test-tube babies and surrogate mothers and frozen embryos and fertility drugs, you meddlesome doctors have complicated a process which most people find admirably simple.'

'Well, AID would be equally effective if we simply put both parties in a pitch-dark room and let them impregnate *per viam naturalem*.'

'That happens,' Sandra murmured.

'Oh, AID's a thriving leisure activity,' I agreed. 'There was something recently in the *BMJ*. Research on the population's blood groups proved that one child in three couldn't remotely have been the husband's.'

I guffawed. She raised her eyebrows. I observed, 'I hope ours are the other two,' but she did not seem to share Imogen's bubbling sense of humour.

The telephone rang. It was Mrs Iles, hysterical.

'I'd better go,' I muttered hurriedly, reaching for my bag.

'But you haven't finished your lunch. What's the matter with the woman?'

'I don't know. She just kept screaming "Come at once!" Maybe she's aborting. She was the one full of the joy of artificial sex.'

'There's apple pie, with cream for a treat.'

But a doctor's duty comes first.

'The childless Ileses lived near the randy Watsons and the hungry Haymasons. They had a newly built colonial-style open-plan house with swimming pool, floodlit patio and brick-housed barbecue. Mr Iles was pacing beside the pool, pulling his hair and beating his chest.

I asked anxiously, 'Some complication of pregnancy?'

He grabbed my lapels, eye-rolling. 'Complications!' he spluttered. 'Look!'

I observed through the double-glazing Mrs Iles on the G-plan sofa, ashen-faced and open-mouthed. On the Parker-Knoll opposite lounged a pale spotty youth wearing tight shiny black leather trousers, Guinness T-shirt, one gold earring, two swastika tattoos and a coiffure like a pink-haired Red Indian, smoking a cigarette with the air of owning the place.

I slid aside the patio doors.

'Who are you?' I demanded fiercely.

He looked round casually. 'You gotta be the bleedin doctor.'

'What right have you to sit there?' I continued sternly.

'Since you ask, mate, I've as much right as our beloved Queen to sit on er frone. I'm the father of this old bird's child, see.'

Mrs Iles put her hands to her cheeks and screamed.

'Impossible!' I stated.

'No it ain't,' he remarked calmly. 'I did a break-in at that wank doctor's place. Purely from idle curiosity, gemme? Meantersay, you give someone somefink useful, you wanna know it's not bin wasted, OK? I found papers wiv all the names on.'

'Is this some devilish blackmail?'

'Now waita minnit. Ain't accusing me of dishonesty, aryer? I might not like that. And when I don't like somefink I'm likely to get *really* roused, see?'

He flicked open a knife from his trouser pocket. Mrs Iles screamed again and fainted.

I put her head between her knees. Mr Iles shook his fists and cried, 'My God, the shock's killed her! You swine! You've murdered a mother and child at one go.' The visitor poured himself a large Scotch from the repro-Tudor cocktail cabinet.

I took her shoulders. Mr Iles took her feet. We carried her upstairs and lay her moaning on their circular bed in the fully fitted mirrored bedroom. I scribbled a prescription for tranquillizers.

'What shall I do?' asked Mr Iles agitatedly.

'Administer TLC.'

'What's that?'

'Tender Loving Care. Useful treatment when all else fails, thus widely practised.'

The youth had lit a large cigar and was pouring a second Scotch.

'I'm calling the police,' I announced resolutely.

'Go on?' he remarked off-handedly.

'You'll be locked up in one of those short-sharp-shock places for life, if I have anything to do with it.'

'You kiddin?' he suggested.

'Frightening a highly sensitive newly pregnant woman like that. It's criminal.'

He looked as innocent as Orphan Annie.

'Tell me wot I done wrong, guv,' he implored.

'Done wrong,' I exclaimed. 'Egad!'

'Apart from a bit of burglary, like everyone else,' he admitted. 'Care for a Scotch?'

'You've done terrible harm just by appearing here.'

He was pained. 'I'm just claiming my paternity rights, ain't I! No one's said nuffink about my feelings in the matter, I've noticed. No one's come to me and said, "Ow, Kevin, ow delightful, without you we'd never ave got the old cow off the ground." I ave given Mrs Iles of my body, and I definitely ave a 50 per cent interest in the action, I wanna see my offspring's reared proper. Natural instincts. No one's gonna argue with that. If they

133

do, I'll soon effin well change their effin mind for them, geddit?' He flicked his knife again.

I was thinking busily during the declaration of paternal solicitude. 'What's in it for you, young feller?'

'Nuffink. Can't a bloke even say 'ello to a woman wot e's screwed by remote control!

'As you noticed, I'm the bleedin doctor. I wasn't born yesterday.'

He sprawled on the sofa, contentedly exhaling cigar smoke. 'OK. Now I'm one of the family, they gotta keep me in style. Can't ave me going round skint, not when I done the old sod's job for im. Stands to reason.' He reached out and helped himself to a handful of assorted cocktail biscuits.

'So you intend to live here with free Scotch and cigars until the child goes to school, if not gets married?'

'You're learnin,' he complimented me.

I had an inspiration. I crossed the front hall, flicking through my appointments dairy. I dialled the discreet doctor. An answering machine informed me he had left on a month's holiday.

I cursed. I paused reflectively on the parquet. It needed a cool professional mind. It struck me, as it did Lady Macbeth, that what's done cannot be undone. Mr Iles came stumbling downstairs, glassy-eyed. I invited him to discuss the unfortunate situation on the patio. He nodded, absently picking up a packet of baby rusks.

'We must be constructive,' I began.

'All right. How?'

'I have taken a detached view of your emotional predicament, and found the only answer,'

'Wonderful!' he exclaimed, mouth full of baby rusks.

'First, you've got to face it. That pink-haired punk is the father of your child. It's inescapable.'

He howled, beating his fist into his palm and scattering rusks over the crazy paving.

'Unfortunately, that's no crime. It was by invitation. I suppose you could nail him for trespassing, but if you took him to court he'd retreat using your dirty washing for flying colours.'

'Every time I look at him I want to fumigate the furniture.'

'People do seem to take their maternity, paternity, gay and lesbian rights so seriously these days. Look at those American tennis players.'

Mr Iles muttered impatiently, 'As we can't simply return his donation with thanks, what next?'

I pronounced, 'Probably the wisest course is for you and Thelma to adopt him.'

Mr Iles tried to push me into the pool.

I felt this a poor reward for imaginative and logical thinking. I bid him good afternoon. I was eager to enjoy my apple pie.

21

Rebuffed, I determined to leave the broody Ileses in their nest with the live-in cuckoo. Overnight, I reflected that I had precipitated a genetic mess which could not be cleaned up, but might be swept decently under the carpet. It was Saturday, with a busy morning surgery. I applied constructive thought while enjoying my fat-free cottage cheese and low-calorie yoghurt.

The telephone rang. It was Mr Iles, hysterical.

'I'd better go,' I muttered hurriedly, reaching for my bag.

'But you haven't finished your lunch. What's the matter with the man?'

'I don't know. Maybe she's swallowed a month's supply of tranquillizers.'

Sandra reminded mc, 'You're playing golf with Jack Windrush at two.'

I reached for my clubs as well. 'I'll drive straight on, unless it's inconveniently fatal.'

Through the half-open patio door I observed Mr and Mrs Iles, Kevin and a teenage girl with green hair.

'It's the bleedin doctor again,' Kevin greeted me amiably, waving his Havana. 'Must be ard up, goin round toutin for custom.'

'Who are you?' I demanded ferociously of the female.

'She's my wife,' Kevin supplied. 'Common-law.'

'Hiya.' She took the cigarette from her mouth. 'Christ, the bleedin fags in this ouse taste of sawdust.'

'Get out,' I ordered, pointing helpfully.

'I ain't gonna leave me usband,' she objected shrilly. 'Not likely. Oojer fink you are, splittin up families?'

'Partickerlary,' Kevin pointed out, 'as Karen's auntie to my unborn baby.'

Mrs Iles broke her silence with hysterical screaming, but happily avoided a faint.

'Edgar, pour a large Scotch for the doctor,' Kevin commanded.

'I am going to tie the barbecue round my neck and jump into the pool,' Mr Iles declared, beating his head with his fists.

'Calm down, everybody,' I directed sternly. 'The relationships of Mrs Iles' coming child are admittedly complex. Doubtless they can be clarified after the happy event. Possibly the College of Heralds can be of help. Meanwhile, the situation calls for constructive thought. Now listen – oh, Edgar, do take Thelma upstairs and stop her screaming. I'll meet you on the patio. Thank you. Now listen, you pair of died-in-the-hair villains,' I continued when we were alone. 'You're not going to use this place as an up-market dosshouse, even if Kevin's impregnated Mrs Iles with sextuplets.'

'Oo, ark at im!' Karen giggled. 'Language!'

'Reely, I'm surprised at you, talking like that,' said Kevin hurtfully. 'I ave a delicate and beautiful relationship wiv Thelma, OK? Can't deny it, neither me nor er. But wot do you suppose me own lovely wife finks about it? Wot would your wife fink, if you came in one night and said, "Ho, by the way me old darlin, hi ham to be the father of another woman's child"?'

'That's an utterly outrageous comparison.'

Karen giggled again. 'Wouldn't put it past im, randy lot of sods them doctors, you'd never believe wot that one in Camden Town did to me, said I'd go blind otherwise, the cheek. Mind, e looked more like a witchdoctor if you ask me.'

I declared in exasperation, 'Your lovely wife thinks exactly as you do – now you've serviced Mrs Iles, you want to extract the largest possible stud fee.'

'Well, we've nowhere else to go,' Kevin pointed out with finality. 'Unless you'd like to take us in? Maybe I can do the same favour for your own old woman, if she ain't well past it?'

I told him what I thought of him.

'Oooo!' cried Karen, hands over ears. 'Whereja suppose e learned words like that?'

Mr Iles was distractedly pacing the patio. I kept him between me and the pool.

'I've got to adopt her as well, I suppose?' he demanded angrily. 'Why not their whole bloody families at the same time, save a lot of bother as they're liable to move in by the busload any moment.'

'Relax, relax.' I gripped his elbow. 'I smell a cellarful of rats. Dial 999.'

'Not on your Nelly.'

I was startled. 'Don't you and Thelma want to stand at the front gate waving your handkerchiefs while they're driven off in a van with flashing blue lights?'

'No.'

'All right, then consult some crafty solicitor. Do you know, there's nothing whatever in the law to stop an AID mother claiming a court order to unmask the father and getting maintenance for life? Any hint of Kevin paying a penny for his own child, he'd be off quicker than a dirty nappie.'

'You and your constructive thought,' he complained bitterly. 'If I had them arrested for anything from blackmail to squatting, all would come out in open court. You said as much yourself. I've told the entire biscuit factory the baby is all my own work. What will they think if I stand in the witness box and confess my pathetic lack of virility? It would have a disastrous effect on labour relations, for a start.'

I countered, 'What's the Kevin pustule do all day in the house?'

'Drink and watch telly.'

'Let's leave them for a bit, while we think even more constructively. After all, they'll be no more trouble about the place than a pair of Great Danes.'

He said doubtfully, 'But my poor wife suffers vomiting of pregnancy – she throws up every time she sets eyes on this awful youth.'

'Send her home to Mother,' I suggested brightly.

'But what about me? I want to vomit whenever I look at him, too.'

I prescribed a pregnancy anti-emetic for them both. I was eager to enjoy my golf.

A week passed. I played golf with Jack Windrush again. On my way home, I called on the Ileses. My meals not having been disturbed by further frenzied phone calls, I assumed the spare pair of parents had been shed.

They were all four enjoying a hot dinner, with a bottle of Blue Nun.

I slipped through the patio doors.

'Why, the doctor,' Mr Iles called cheerfully above the laughter. 'Kevin, my dear lad, pour him a Scotch. Karen, love, help Thelma to more stuffing and take another slice for yourself. Excuse me if I go and have a little consultation on the patio.'

'Are you euphoric?' I demanded outside. 'Like hostages who fawn on their captors?'

'I decided temporarily to accept the situation,' he explained. 'Like Sindbad the Sailor with the Old Man of the Sea on his back. And after all,' he reflected, 'Kevin and Karen aren't such bad youngsters at heart.'

'Personally, I think they make Bonnie and Clyde look like the Bisto kids.'

'Maybe they're just misunderstood at home, by society and so on,' he continued dreamily. 'It's quite unrealistic, expecting everyone in the world to behave as if they were members of Churchford Golf Club. They've simply been deprived of cultural opportunities. Thelma and I are already planning visits to the public library, antique boutiques, the local ruins. Yes, they're a jolly, lively pair, once you get to know them,' he revealed. 'Full of fun and good-natured teasing. And it makes a change, young laughter echoing through the house, even at all hours of the day and night. When the infant arrives,' he ended determinedly, 'we'll be just one happy, integrated family, though mind you, their language is terrible, and you cannot leave so much as a second-class postage stamp around or they nick it.'

'You're mad,' I exploded. 'Don't you realize, this callous couple of crooks will lounge about freeloading until they're bored, then scarper with everything in the house not actually fixed down with six-inch screws? Probably invite some of their equally jolly and lively young friends to come and help themselves.'

'If only somebody would tell me what to do,' he said pathetically.

'I keep telling you what to do.'

'I mean, tell me what to do that I wanted to do.'

'Bribe them,' I suggested constructively. 'You must be worth a bob or two? Everyone munches biscuits, even in world recessions.'

'Wouldn't they just spend the money and come back?' He wiped away a tear. 'I've nothing left but a brave face. This is a situation totally unknown in the history of parenthood since the Garden of Eden.'

I left. I was eager to enjoy my evening Glenfiddich.

The following weekend Mrs Iles appeared at evening surgery.

'Thought I'd better have a check-up, doctor, to see the baby's unaffected by that nasty experience.'

'Ha! They've taken their leave?'

'Didn't you hear?' She was amazed. 'It's all round Churchford, five in the morning police arrived, hundreds of them, with walkie-talkies and Alsatians, surrounded the house and took them off in handcuffs, it was better than the telly.' She sat across the consulting desk like a cat which had had a narrow escape but still counted nine lives. 'It was all a con job, you see, they burgled my doctor in Wimpole Street, stole his appointments book, and used it to terrify families all over the Home Counties until they were bought off. Edgar won't even need stand up in court. They're wanted for a whole catalogue of crimes from grievous bodily harm to shoplifting.'

I exclaimed, 'What a worry lifted for both of us! And now your baby's parentage will remain an inviolate secret for ever and ever. Amen!'

Andy had arrived home for dinner. I opened a bottle of Bruichladdich.

'How's Imogen?'

'Ah, Imogen. We decided we were incompatible. It was all perfectly amiable. When we parted, she said she would give me first refusal of her kidneys on her donor card.'

Briefly condoling, I leaned against the mantelpiece to recount with relish the Ileses' pregnancy drama.

Andy grinned. 'The Wimpole Street wank bank! I think all the donors are medical students.'

'Medical students! A turn-off for the prospective mothers, isn't it?'

'Ah, the vulgar Dickens' Bob Sawyer image,' Andy corrected me.

'Even the refined Thackeray called medical students rakish, gallant, dashing and dirty.'

'Well, didn't we play up to it, Dad, both of us? It was fun, made us exciting to girls, and perhaps the horrors wouldn't have been tolerable otherwise. Medical students are highly responsible young persons, or they wouldn't be let in. *And* they know all about hereditary diseases. Did you hear that Italian women are mad on English medics? Well, on their sperm. Just imagine the Ileses' situation in reverse – some twenty-year-old Italian raver invading a middle-aged doctors' conference in London demanding Daddy?'

I laughed heartily.

'Must have made a useful few quid out of Wimpole Street, when I was a student,' he reflected nostalgically.

'You?'

'Yes, my specimens were frozen. Funny thing, I ran into the sperm-mongering doctor at St Swithin's about a couple of months ago, and he mentioned he was just getting round to using my donations.'

Sandra entered as my whisky glass crashed to the hearth.

'What's the matter?' she exclaimed in alarm.

'I am Mrs Iles' baby's grandfather,' I told her. 'What's for dinner?'

22

Christmas is coming, and I still have not retired.

From a shop long remembered behind Edinburgh Castle, I ordered a case of selected single malts – Auchentoshan, Inchgower, Dalwhinnie, Tullibardine, Ladyburn, Craigellachie, Rosebank, Bunnahabhain. Lovely names. Lovely whisky.

It arrived at breakfast-time.

'You mustn't drink too much over Christmas,' Sandra uttered the routine warning.

'As every medical student knows, alcohol dilates the coronary arteries.'

'I can't understand why you tipple so. The whole family for Christmas dinner should be stimulating enough. Everyone knows what a scream my brother George is.'

'I'll tell you why.' I screwed up my eyes. 'I quote the Victorian novelist Marcus Clarke – "Pleasing images flock to my brain, the fields break into flower, the birds into song, the sea gleams sapphire, the warm heaven laughs. Great God! what man could withstand a temptation like this?" Mind, he was writing about an alcoholic parson on an Australian convict settlement.'

Sandra silently cleared away breakfast, unmoved by English literature.

It was a bleak Monday morning. The young Bellwethers, married last autumn, arrived at the surgery with a dead cat.

They unwrapped it from the *Guardian* on my consulting desk, cold and stiff. It appeared a sad case of feline hypothermia.

'Spent the night in our deep-freeze,' Herbert Bellwether informed me solemnly.

The tragedy flashed upon my mind like the apocalypse. The couple delving for the oven-ready chips, tabby inflamed by the unleashed tang of fish fingers, the lid carelessly slammed, piteous miaows unheard, supper eaten and telly watched, fruitless puss-pusses throughout their little home, with the breakfast bacon stark revelation.

'Rotten luck,' I sympathized. 'Though the end was probably painless.'

'I mean, the body spent the night in our deep-freeze.'

I was puzzled. 'Wouldn't you be better off calling at the vet's? Though it rather looks as if nothing can be done at this stage.'

'This cat is a doctor's problem cat,' he insisted quietly.

I started. Rabies! It was raging chronically among cross-Channel cats. From Boulogne to Bordeaux people were frothing at the mouth and shying at their bottles of Perrier. I recalled posters at the ports more intimidating than the Customs men, and coastal magistrates regretful at an inability to have pet smugglers put down.

'Who's it bitten?' I demanded anxiously.

'Can't you see, doctor?' Julie Bellwether pointed tearfully. 'She's been shot in the neck.'

'How extraordinary. It's nice of you to let me have a look, but I'd suggest you display the corpse to the RSPCA. They must be hot stuff on feline murder.'

'It happened at the General Hospital,' Herbert added.

I became lost in a blizzard of bewilderment.

The Bellwethers had been my patients since childhood. Herbert wore a beard and an anorak and ran a garden centre. Julie had straight hair and big round glasses and helped at a nursery school. They were an ideally suited gentle couple, who believed the world would be a better place if it renounced nuclear weapons and ate compost-grown veg.

I inquired, 'Some disturbed patient ran amok with an automatic? I do hope he did not similarly shoot his psychiatrist?'

'On Sunday afternoon they had a cat shootout,' Herbert explained.

'I don't think I follow?'

'You know we live right against the hospital? Well, a man appeared beyond our back garden fence with a rifle and started firing at cats. He got six, including Samantha.'

I mentioned, 'Do you think we might have the cat wrapped up again? Thank you so much.'

'She was in such lovely condition,' said Julie anguishedly. 'I cry every time I see her unopened tins of cat food.'

'But surely someone must have noticed a man spending his Sunday afternoon going round shooting cats?'

'They certainly did, doctor!' Herbert said indignantly. 'There was a really nasty scene when the porters and cooks at the General twigged what was going on. They loved those cats, doctor, as we loved our Samantha.'

He described vividly domestic staff attacking the mass murderer with brooms, stretcher poles, frying pans and choppers, forcing him to flee in his van leaving his prey scattered round the consultants' car park. The corpses had been cherished for months in the hospital kitchens, lavished with scraps and saucers of creamy milk, bedded down cosily among the central-heating pipes. It was hardly less horrible than a man going round to shoot the geriatric patients.

'But why pepper a pack of pussies?' I asked. 'For coat collars? Chinese restaurant delicacies? Was he a nostalgic tiger hunter? Had he a thing about cats, like Napoleon?'

'Search me.' Herbert shrugged. 'That's why we hoped you'd help us, doctor. Nothing can bring our Samantha back, but she might prevent other cats suffering the same end.'

I agreed reluctantly, 'Oh, all right. I'll phone Mr Applebee, the administrator at the General, about the fiendish carnage. Meanwhile, would you please ensure that the cat is unnoticed as you pass through the waiting room? Or I shall have to have the place fumigated, at great expense.'

I had not met Applebee since our involvement with the bodyscanner in question. It took two days to reach him – such remoteness is a common hazard with persons in administration, to display their overwork and give them a chance to guess what the devil you are after. The delay stoked my indignation, until I felt towards the incident much as Milton towards the Late Massacre in Piedmont, and started with the conversational equivalent of *Avenge, O Lord! They slaughter'd Saints.*

'Shooting cats is part of official National Health Service policy,' he countered stiffly.

'Simpleton that I am,' I apologized. 'Some *Dummkopf* might similarly have phoned the *Führerbunker* inquiring why the Nazis gassed people.'

'Really, Dr Gordon, you're not being helpful or even sympathetic towards the exhausting difficulties we face administering the NHS,' he returned severely. 'Cats are a major problem. Worse than fiddled meat invoices, the disappearing floor-polish mountain and typewriters going like giveaway ballpoints. Don't you realize, the General hosts a colony of fifty feral cats? So does every one of the five thousand hospitals in the country. This equals a quarter of a million untamed cats eating their heads off at the expense of the Health Service, which as everyone knows is tighter for cash than the Church of England. And further, Dr Gordon, let me tell you the cats are using my heating ducts as a vast litter tray, the engineers are complaining the basement is alive with cat fleas, they are threatening to strike and bring the hospital to a total halt any minute, all because the sentimental domestic staff lavish tender loving care on vermin which are now learning to jump through the windows after the patients' dinners. I've had terrible scenes in the wards, people screaming and waving their scratches, two patients are already suing me and the marksman's boss becomes perfectly abusive on the telephone about experts being insulted and assaulted by ignorant kitchen-hands, who are refusing to work while they organize stretcher parties to bring in survivors wounded in action.'

He paused.

'I appreciate you have an ecology problem,' I conceded. 'But surely you could find a less sensational means of curbing your annoyance than occurred to the late A Capone on St Valentine's Day?'

'Cats are a health hazard,' he replied firmly. 'My duty is to summon the pest-control people, and if a .22 rifle is their most effective instrument, who am I to disagree? Do you expect mc to tell surgeons to use fingers instead of scalpels? Listen, when the Great Exhibition opened in London in 1851, sparrows got into the brand-new glittering Crystal Palace, twittering everywhere and doing things on the top hats and furbelows. Queen Victoria was not amused at all. But she knew the man for the job – the ancient Duke of Wellington, who advised at once, "Sparrowhawks, ma'am." It was as great a success as the Battle of Waterloo. This country must be ruthlessly businesslike, or it goes under. Satisfied?'

'Why not put in ferrets?' I suggested, but he had rung off.

The Bellwethers were back the following week. Bits of *Guardian* now stuck to the cat's fur, like thermal underwear to the lost body of an Arctic hero.

'It's happening in hospitals all over,' said Herbert sombrely, handing me some cuttings. I felt a duty towards the Health Service of holding a glimmer of reason to the misty-eyed dissidents, but he interrupted determinedly, 'And I'm going to stop it, doctor.'

'Isn't there some pressure group for promoting the welfare of poor, helpless cats?' inquired Julie meekly.

'Undoubtedly. There is for promoting the welfare of everything else in the country from smokers to beer-drinkers.' I thought. 'PUSSY! That's it. Always in the newspapers. Why not phone them and state your case? No knowing where it will end – questions in Parliament, Court of Human Rights, the Esther Rantzen show.'

They thanked me heart-warmingly, wrapped up the cat and left.

There were only three shopping days to Christmas. The Bellwethers reappeared.

'Very sensible of you, transferring the cat to a black bin-liner,' I congratulated them. It was frosty-furred and fossil-hard, and rattled on the consulting desk. 'How did you get on with PUSSY?'

'It was a bit funny,' Herbert reported awkwardly. 'The lady said, "Why don't you walk round King's Cross yourself, dearie, and chat up some of the girls?"

'PUSSY's not for cats,' Julie explained. 'It's for something else.'

I apologized, 'With so many people so busy living up to their acronyms, a slight muddle is excusable.' I remembered, 'CAT! The Cat Action Trust. Ring up the lady in charge of that. Good thing the gaffe wasn't made vice versa.'

They thanked me sincerely, shrouded Samantha and left. They returned the following morning. I implored them forcefully not to let the

146

cat out of the bag. It was getting like the pheasant which Rollo Basingstoke sent us, which lay forgotten under the dog food for three years.

Julie began excitedly, 'The CAT people were terribly interested. They said the Ministry gunfire was utterly deplorable.'

'They'd a much better idea,' Herbert added enthusiastically. 'Trap the cats, neuter them, and put them back again.'

'You see, that doesn't create a cat vacuum,' Julie pointed out.

'To be filled by a new wave of cats,' Herbert amplified.

'So the neutered cats live there happily, until they disappear by natural wastage,' Julie ended with satisfaction.

I charitably promised to pass the survival plan to Applebee. I took the chance of mentioning that Samantha was possibly due for decent interment, the smell causing curiosity, even alarm, in the waiting room, and could not be doing their dairy ice cream and frozen peas much good.

Herbert gave a dark look. 'We are keeping her above ground, doctor, because we are planning direct action.'

I wished them a Merry Christmas.

I caught Applebee on Christmas Eve. Over the telephone, I urged in the spirit of the season the CAT alternative.

'After all,' I emphasized, 'it's better to be castrated than catsmeat.'

'How the hell are we going to neuter a quarter of a million cats?' he objected. 'Do you realize, there are more than a million feral cats in the country, the population of Birmingham? Why, the sterilizers would be more overworked than the NHS junior doctors. And perhaps you would tell me how I'm to catch the cats? Particularly as they may not much care for the operation.'

I demurred.

'Would you?' he asked.

'Why not dig pitfalls, baiting them with mice? They work splendidly for elephants.'

But he found it no more amusing than Queen Victoria the sparrows. I decided he was the voice of humourless, heartless officialdom, and hoped the cat would vanish from my life after Christmas as Marley's ghost from Scrooge's.

I was in paper hat carving the turkey for my extended family in the middle of Christmas Day when the doorbell rang. I cursed. On the mat was Applebee, distraught. He was holding hands with Julie. She was holding hands with Herbert. Applebee was also holding the cat, gift-wrapped in holly paper. I was confused.

Applebee cried, 'We're stuck!'

Julie giggled. 'With Superglue.'

Herbert chuckled. 'Mr Applebee opened his front door thinking he was getting a nice present, and now we're all firm friends. Including Samantha.'

I asked Applebee shortly, 'What do you expect me to do about it?'

'Dissolve us,' he demanded hysterically. 'Surely you've some sort of antidote? You must always be getting teenagers with noses stuck into plastic bags inhaling the stuff. All my wife's relatives are getting famished. How can anyone carve a turkey attached to a dead cat?'

I grabbed the cat and pulled. I found I was adhered, too. Sandra opened the dining-room door, curious about the spectre at the feast. I politely introduced her. She shook hands with Herbert, and became stuck. My son Andy and daughter Jilly emerged, puzzled. Also George, Bill and Augustus (their uncles), Sal, Mary and Janet (aunts) and Hilda (widowed same). 'Keep clear!' I yelled.

Instantly assuming the cat was emitting a highly infectious plague, they clapped hands over their mouths and cowered behind the Christmas tree. Andy bravely pulled at the cat, and got stuck. Uncle George rang the fire brigade. We sat on the floor, awaiting the arrival of the appliances. I remarked to Applebee, 'Why, I've solved your cat problem! Simply present each patient with a complimentary cat to take home from hospital.'

Applebee scowled. The man had no sense of humour even on Christmas Day.

23

In the New Year we held a party. My daughter had become Miss Gordon.

Jilly had passed her Fellowship of the Royal College of Surgeons, who display supreme professional snobbery by shedding the title 'doctor'. She conceded that Daddy was right. Surgery was a masculine career, like conducting orchestras and bookmaking. She was refocusing on gynaecology. As Bertie's registrar job was shortly vacant at the General, Jilly suggested it would be smart to invite the Taverills, and to make sure also to ask their son Peter, who was already halfway up the golden gynaecological ladder in London as senior registrar at the Royal Women's.

Over my Laphroaig I informed Bertie of that morning's patient Ms Clew, who, being liberated, wished to give birth under water.

'How tiresome.' He spiked the olive from his martini with the same elegant, neat gesture that he used when inserting a stitch into a lady's intimate parts. 'I'm utterly exasperated by women who read smart articles in the Sunday papers and demand to give birth in peculiar positions. What did you tell her?'

'That it was fine for mermaids.'

Ms Clew was a big comprehensive schoolmistress, seven months gone in a macramé smock. I did not enlighten Bertie with her response to my suggestion that she invoked his expert care at the General.

'No thank *you*,' she had complained, red spots on pale cheeks. 'I've already had two there, and they treat the mothers as suffering from a disease called pregnancy, when childbirth should be an experience of astonishing beauty and sensuality, as that lady said on television. They put you in the stranded beetle position and fire everyone off with drugs every morning like a barrage of guns. All this high technology! Why can't I enjoy natural childbirth in my own home?'

An upset patient means a bad doctor.

'My dear Ms Clew,' I had said soothingly. 'Giving birth is not just another wifely domestic duty like cooking the Sunday roast. Believe me, Ms Clew, doctors entertain the same caring feelings towards labouring mothers as lifeboat men to shipwrecked mariners, and will similarly spare no effort to bring them safely through the harrowing experience, but obviously the lifesavers must use the most efficient lifeboat, the latest safety gadgets, and expect the floundering sailors to obey the megaphoned instructions for their own good. See?'

Slightly mollified, she muttered something about male obstetricians feeling threatened at losing the birthing process. She informed me, 'Well, I'm taking my case to Re-Birth, in Islington. They're very concerned about the sexual exploitation of women in labour.'

I am not impressed with the women's liberation movement. A lifetime in medicine develops a sensitive nose for the whiff of bullshit in the winds of change.

Bertie Taverill was a handsome man with bristly grey hair and expensive suits. He was inclined like many consultants to be unthinkingly condescending towards us poor bloody GPs, though careful to keep on our right side, as we supplied the raw material for his rich tapestry of life.

'I should hate to perform a delivery under water,' he remarked. 'A newborn baby's a slippery little thing, I might lose it like the soap in the bath. How nice to see Jilly looking so happy.'

'If you're not happy as a young hospital doctor, you never will be.'

'My Peter seems to be seeing a lot of her.'

I looked blank.

'Oh, he's always taking her out to theatres and dinner in London. Well, you can't expect children to tell Mummy and Daddy everything when they've got an FRCS. Eh, eh?'

He laughed heartily and dug me in the ribs hard (with the tips of two fingers, you could tell he was a gynaecologist).

I bore the news to Sandra under the pretence of offering nuts. Her eyes glowed over her Tio Pepe. Young Taverill, across the room chatting to Dr Lonelyhearts, was good-looking, well off and clever, and having a gynaecologist as your daughter's boyfriend is somehow reassuring, like letting a racing driver borrow the family car.

I mentioned Peter to Jilly over the washing-up.

'Oh, yes, I have been out with him once or twice. I thought it useful, talking to someone at my own level about the career prospects in gynae,' she explained over the sink. 'Did you know he's already invented a new method of laparoscopic sterilization? He's dreadfully brainy and frighteningly hard-working, it's a wonder he manages to be so terribly nice and have such delightfully civilized manners and be so well dressed, he has a remarkable knowledge of books and music and is an absolutely fascinating conversationalist and is terribly sophisticated in restaurants and drives a Lotus.'

'This is only a professional relationship?' I hazarded.

'Oh, definitely. I'm keeping in with the Taverill family only to further my career, which of course comes first.'

'Admirable,' I agreed heartily. 'Well, mine's over. I'm retiring.'

'No! But you'll be bored, like some resting old Shakespearean actor.'

'So your mother said,' I told her wearily. 'Luckily, I've hit on an agreeable retirement activity. Literature!'

'You mean, you're actually going to write that book you keep talking about, on twenty-five years in general practice?'

'Even if I publish it at my own expense, by what they call "vanity presses". Though Dr Lonelyhearts once told me,' I reflected, 'that all presses were vanity presses – he knew a lot of authors.'

The idea was sharpened by discovering in my shelves an ancient copy of *Dr Bradley Remembers*, by (Dr) Francis Brett Young, a novel I had read as an impressionable student. Its hero was a family doctor pre-NHS – at first, even pre-L1 G – shabby in traditional frock coat and wing collar, practising in a grotty Midland town with gas-lit consulting room and oilskin-covered couch, wrapping beautifully his self-dispensed medicines with dabs of scarlet wax, recalling his professional life on his retirement eve at seventy-three, beloved by his old patients and scorned by his new colleagues, his wife dead in childbirth, his son not only dying from morphine addiction but failing his finals as well, and arthritis in both hips. A blub a page, I now adjudged, rereading it in bed. The night after the party I reached the final paragraph. Dr Bradley is called to his last case.

The rain drummed fiercely on the top of his opened umbrella. The little girl nestled close to his side and clung to his left arm as she had been bidden. They passed, that odd pair, across the rain-slashed oblong of light that the window cast.

You can almost see the credit titles rolling up, I thought contemptuously, turning out the bedside light. I could surely do better than such unrealistic sentimental rubbish!

I decided next morning I must break to my partners the sad news of my retirement. At the surgery front door I encountered Elaine Spondeck.

'What a splendid idea!' she responded. 'Did you know, Richard, I've thought of suggesting it for months? You so obviously hate plodding along with the burden of the practice. Indeed, the three of us had long discussions how we could tactfully suggest that such self-sacrifice was deeply appreciated, but unnecessary. Why, now we can take in some bright, up-to-date, dead keen young doctor who'll do most of the work for us all.'

I withdrew to my consulting room with mixed feelings.

'Mrs Jenkins,' I announced solemnly as she followed with the letters. 'I am going to retire.'

'Oh, good!' she exclaimed. 'You know, I'm absolutely dying to spend my life at home tending my garden and husband, but obviously I couldn't while still needing to tend you. I mean, all the patients know how delightfully vague you are about things like sick notes and repeat prescriptions and cremation certificates. When are you leaving, exactly? Resigning end of month, then taking due holiday? I'll type my own resignation right after morning surgery.'

I sat staring across my consulting desk, torn between feeling that I should have vanished long ago to universal acclaim or should stay until senility to teach them a lesson.

I was interrupted by my first patient, Moira Days, twenty-six, pale and pretty, who wished to distribute all her organs.

'I saw it in the paper, doctor, how someone gave his heart and his kidneys, and his liver, I rather fancy. It is my wish to bestow the same upon humanity, and I wondered if any others were transferable.'

I mentioned corneas, though adding encouragingly, 'At the end of your own long life, Moira, perhaps we'll assemble an entire human-being construction kit. You never know, with these ambitious surgeons. But why the sudden generosity?'

'Well, I've nothing in life which means anything but my little Tracey.'

She was a clean, solemn, fair child of six, sitting beside mother quietly reading Snoopy.

'And I'd like to feel I'd done some good, passing through this world. Who knows? My kidneys might live after me in some man doing great deeds, like a Member of Parliament. Or maybe end up in a real saint like a bishop.'

'How's things at home?' I asked.

She could smile as she said, 'My husband's gone away again, six years this time, robbery with violence; still, it spares me getting knocked about for a bit, doesn't it? My old dad's no better in that home with his stroke, and you know about my mum in the bin, my brother's into hard drugs now, heroin and that, and my sister's still on the game, though she pretends she's a hostess and attracts rich Arabs. Well, it could be worse. We could all be dead.'

I was constantly amazed at Moira. She was left in perfectly good shape by the mills of fate, which would have rolled me flat as tinplate.

'If only half my patients kept as sunny with one-hundredth of your troubles,' I congratulated her.

'I always remember what Dad told me from some radio show back in the war – "It's being so cheerful as keeps me going." '

'By the way, I'm retiring at the end of January.'

'No! You mustn't.' She added shyly, 'You're the only doctor I want to look after me.'

'All doctors have the same training, you know,' I pointed out.

'You're the only one I really trust.'

'I assure you that my three partners are extremely trustworthy,' I rebuked her mildly.

'But it's you who's kept me off the drink.' Now her face clouded. 'I'm always remembering the terrible time I had.' She shuddered. 'It's horrible, just the thought of slipping back.'

I gently pooh-poohed my importance in her eyes, but I was deeply stirred. Perhaps I should stay after all? But it would be such a dreadful disappointment to Mrs Jenkins.

24

Mr Clew at morning surgery, bubble-haired, droopy-moustached, velvet-jacketed, interior decorating and fitted kitchens. He announced that he would deliver the baby at home himself.

'That will really open a tin of wasps,' I predicted forcefully.

'But if giving birth is not a family matter, what is?' He was one of those irritatingly aggressive meek people, who wish to inherit the earth without delay. 'Debbie and me are a serene, caring couple, and it occurs to me that women were having babies long before doctors were invented. I saw our two little ones being delivered at the General, and I must say there seemed nothing to it.'

'It's the same with showjumping on the telly. Looks as easy as riding the roundabouts, until you try it yourself.'

'Haven't human beings something deep down to produce their young safely, like the rest of God's animals, doctor? I don't think I've seen anything more tender than a cow with a newborn calf or a mare with a foal. When the time comes, won't the father's instinct work as strongly as the mother's? Debbie and me vibrate as one person, you know. So powerfully that when she goes into labour I develop stomach pains.'

'The couvade is a well-recognized male reaction to childbirth,' I informed him briskly. 'I believe there was a lot of it about among the Red Indians.'

He made the hushed suggestion, 'Why don't *you* deliver my wife, doctor, at home? Surely you're entitled to?'

'I'm entitled to do heart transplants, but for the good of all concerned I prefer leaving them to doctors who know more about it than I do. Well, if you want to deliver your wife's child, I can't stop you, no more than cutting her corns. Good morning.'

I reached home for lunch to find Dr Basil Barty-Howells, the new consultant physician at the General, who everyone tells me is utterly brilliant, standing on my hearthrug in an agitated state.

'Look, about the Queen opening our brand-new Elizabeth Block in three weeks,' he said, accepting a barely noticeable sherry.

'It isn't brand-new.'

'Buildings unlike ships can be launched when going full speed ahead,' he remarked impatiently. 'Oh, I know it was started when Barbara Castle was Minister of Health, or perhaps Enoch Powell, but those little problems like having to redig the foundations, the asbestos lagging likely to kill all the patients and the plastic ceilings liable to burn like napalm, and the unions blacking the improved food trolleys, they're happening to new hospitals throughout the NHS. It's an opening to celebrate, that's why we asked all the local GPs. Particularly when the rest of the General resembles a cross between a Victorian abattoir and a refugee camp. I was to make the speech welcoming Her Majesty, but I can't.'

'Stage fright!'

'No, hunting.'

'Couldn't you put it off?'

He began to pace the room. 'As a student, I was a dedicated anti-huntsman. I sabotaged them all. Had wonderful days out with the Quorn, Pytchley, Heythrop! So I cannot bring myself to address the mother of a regular hunter. Oh, I know it's ridiculous.' He shakingly set down his untasted sherry. 'But I suffer overwhelming feelings of revulsion. As everyone knows, I'm a socialist anti-nuclear ecologist.'

I nodded. He had a beard.

'So as you're retiring –'

'What! How did you know? I divulged the secret to my partners and receptionist only yesterday.'

'Oh, it's all over Churchford. So we thought it would be a nice gesture for you to do the speech. It would also prevent quite murderous jealousy among the other hospital consultants.'

'Impossible!'

'What, you're a hunt saboteur, too?'

'No, but I'm unaccustomed to public speaking.'

'Nonsense. They tell me at golf club dinners you go on for hours. I'll announce you've accepted. I'm late for my clinic.'

When I bemusedly told Sandra, she said, 'I must buy some more clothes.'

'You've already spent a fortune on clothes.'

'That was for being in the audience, not part of the show. I'll go this very afternoon to Robbins Modes.'

Next morning Mrs Bryanston-Hicks demanded to see me in the surgery. She was Churchford's queen-bee midwife. She was nearly six feet tall, with tits the size of goldfish bowls. She was enough to make any newborn baby bolt back to its burrow. She slapped on my desk the *Churchford Echo*.

She said, 'Well?'

I was appalled. The front page. Mr Clew defying the General Hospital by doing his own thing with his own baby, encouraged by Dr Gordon, one of the few traditional family doctors, full of loving care. There was a big photograph of the family under a sign, CLEW'S CLASSIC KITCHENS.

I pointed out nervously, 'But the *Echo* is no more reliable for the truth than *Pravda*.'

She declared forthrightly, 'I am going to prosecute Mr Clew under the Midwives Act (1951).'

I frowned. 'You can't do that.'

'Of course I can. It's all in section 9.'

'But isn't the Midwives Act only to stop Sara Gamps setting up obstetrical shops in their back rooms?'

'Don't you read the papers? We've brought unruly fathers to heel everywhere from Stockton-on-Tees to Redruth. We can't allow the whole country to have babies however they please, making a mockery of midwives.'

I murmured defensively, 'Mr Clew's a very caring man.'

'Caring, caring!' she exploded. 'Why does everyone these days say caring when they only mean sloppiness? Looking after people is damn tough work demanding a highly trained intellect. Was anybody more

157

caring than Florence Nightingale? Of course not. And what did she do? Rolled up her sleeves and organized everybody, like Mrs Thatcher and the Falklands.'

I complained uneasily, 'That paper's dreadfully unfair. I only said that people needn't take the doctor's medicine or advice if they didn't feel like it. Look at the Jehovah's Witnesses.'

'In that case,' she said, 'I shall prosecute you as well, as an accessory before the fact.'

My horror grew with the winter shadows. I calculated that I could be hauled before the General Medical Council on four counts. Advertising myself in the papers. Inciting lawbreaking. Denigrating my fellow-practitioners at the General. And associating with unqualified midwives. I thanked God for shame avoided by pre-emptive retirement.

I drove home that evening to find Jilly. She said that Bertie Taverill was most surprised at my behaviour, but supposed I was seeking martyrdom like a Russian dissident. He had expressed puzzlement at my knocking his competence, as a fellow-student from St Swithin's, a neighbour who was always furthering my own professional interests, social life and family happiness. He hoped the GMC would take a lenient view, though he could not for the life of him see how they could possibly avoid striking me off for years.

I said unhappily that I hoped it would not upset Peter.

She snapped, 'What do you mean, Peter? I'm only concerned about my career. I mean absolutely nothing to Peter.'

She left the room hurriedly.

The atmosphere in my house was as in Cleopatra's during the application of asps. I bolted to the golf club. In the bar was Dr Quaggy.

'Read all about you in the paper, Richard.'

'Halfway through this morning's surgery, I decided that if another patient said that to me with a sly grin, I would batter him to death with the knee-jerk hammer.'

'As an old friend, Richard, I can tell you frankly we've been worried about your overstrain for months. All the GPs are terribly relieved to hear you're going for good.'

He smiled like a snake in the grass meeting a charmer. 'By a strange coincidence, my son Arnold has just finished that GP training. He would be absolutely ideal to step into your shoes, I'm sure you'll agree? Did you hear I'm becoming president of the Churchford Medical Society, after Charlie Pexham died last year? Not of course that that would influence the selection committee in Arnold's favour. Poor Charlie!' He sighed into his pink gin. 'Should have retired early, might have been alive today. We all miss him.'

I agreed. There were many of my colleagues I passionately wished were not dead, and vice versa.

I drove to the empty, dark surgery. I had to dredge my alluvia on the shoals of time. I tipped my files on to my desk. I was baffled where to start. I supposed Gibbon felt the same about the decline and fall of the Roman Empire.

My mind wandered. I reached for *Titles and Forms of Address*, borrowed from Dr Lonelyhearts. My first problem with the Queen was how to say hello. The book directed me to use 'Ma'am'. But as in ham or marmalade? It added, 'On presentation to the Queen the subject does not start the conversation.'

Just like doctors, I thought, who *always* start the conversation, even if just, 'What, you here again?' The royalty business suddenly lay exposed. Just like doctors, royals must be unflaggingly pleasant to a succession of total strangers not feeling at their best, often embarrassed by the unwonted situation and some possibly pissed.

What do royals think about during a lifetime of interminable addresses by mayors, worshipful masters and bards in Welsh? I wondered. It was humanly impossible to concentrate on the flood of oratory while awaiting your cue to slap trowel on foundation stone, fire champagne at bows, congratulate some university's harvest of intellectual sprouts. I supposed that like the rest of us at boring parties they wondered if the lads were likely to kill themselves with daring sports, the girls were pregnant again, what was for dinner, why the spouse was so bloody-minded this morning and where the money goes.

I composed a few simple sentences on a blank patient's card. The worry about speechifying lessens with not trying to be too clever, as I advise young persons worried about sex. It was midnight. Jilly would be back at the General, Sandra in bed. I could venture home for a solitary soporific single malt.

That night I had a frightful dream. I stood wordless and blank-minded while everyone coughed and shuffled their feet and the Queen eyed me like her predecessor on receiving a newsflash of the approaching Armada. I woke in panic. The anxiety lingered. I could become tongue-tied, lose my notes. We would be Not Amused at my joke. I began to share the phobia of P G Wodehouse's Gussie Fink-Nottle presenting the prizes, of my trousers splitting down the back. I began to wish I had never accepted.

My first patient that morning was Moira Days. She had deposited Tracey early at the nearby Clement Attlee Primary. I wondered if she still wished to leave her mark on our faded insubstantial pageant, even nestling in someone else's pelvis. Though with her alcoholic history. I would not take her liver as a gift.

'Doctor, I can't afford to live in my room just down the road any longer,' she revealed chirpily. 'What with being supportive to my brother, and Dad griping about missing his little comforts in that home, and of course Tracey having to be properly nourished and I won't have her shabbily dressed, it means a lot to a child, I always say, you'd be surprised how cruel they can be to one another in the playground. If I wasn't so cheerful I'd think of letting the Welfare take Tracey and ending it all, honestly.'

I interrupted sharply by quoting Churchill. 'Never commit suicide, you may live to regret it.'

Moira laughed. I was puzzled. 'Doctor, you're always making that joke. Don't worry, the patients often have a good giggle in the waiting room, how you always make the same little jokes to all of us.'

With mixed feelings, I remarked, 'Well, you can enjoy some brand-new jokes from Dr Spondeck, once I retire.'

'Don't say that, doctor.' She fell silent. 'Don't retire yet. Please. You're my only friend left.'

I gently pooh-poohed that I was more than her medical adviser. But I was deeply stirred.

25

My last week in medical practice. My career would end like a Prime Minister's by seeing the Queen.

By the Wednesday morning I felt I would give anything for Basil Barty-Howells to appear saying he was doing it after all. At lunchtime he appeared saying he was doing it after all.

He distractedly paced the carpet. 'This is dreadfully awkward, Richard. I know it's exactly the honour we should all have liked to see marking your retirement, but the Ministry are absolutely insisting that I perform. The government seems to have sunk almost as many millions into the new building as into the North Sea. So they want one of their own doctors to get on television news. Also, the health workers require a glowing tribute from a consultant, or they'll instantly shut the place down again by blacking the improved operating-theatre lifts. And further, I feel fox-hunting is perhaps not so inhibiting, as I'm into gassed badgers.'

I exclaimed, 'Utterly delighted! I've become a terrible case of pedal hypothermia.'

As he left, I imparted to Sandra, 'Hooray! No speech. Now I've absolutely no obligation to retire.'

She stared. 'But all month you've been grumbling about hardly waiting to get out.'

'Ah, yes.' I agreed. 'And so I do. Well, I hope I shall have a nice quiet week, before never again laying hands on human flesh except your own.'

In the waiting room as I arrived for evening surgery was Mrs Radnor. She was neat, slight, thirtyish, with a black eye. Accompanying her was a huge woman in jeans and a fisherman's knit sweater, who announced herself as Ms Hammersham of Sanctuary.

'Ms Radnor is a battered wife,' she informed me. 'I want you to examine her, doctor, before I call the police.'

I barred her following us into the consulting room. 'I examine patients without a studio audience, if you don't mind.'

She glared. 'But I demand to be present. I am safeguarding women's rights.'

I said, 'Hop it, dearie.'

She retired, fuming and muttering about the *Guardian*.

I sat Mrs Radnor down, still in her apron, and asked what happened.

'Well, Fred's tea was cold again, it was egg and chips, and he lost his temper, hardly blame him, really, he hit me in the eye, or perhaps he just caught it with his elbow while making threatening gestures, but I was in a temper myself, and remembered Sanctuary in what used to be the greengrocer's on the corner, so I went straight there, I suppose mostly to get away from Fred, who was carrying on like a great baby, but the big lady got all excited and wants to send Fred to jail.'

I examined the contusion. No treatment needed. We emerged. I explained to Ms Hammersham it was a storm in that afternoon's teacup.

She countered, 'I demand, Dr Gordon, that you supply signed evidence of Ms Radnor's violation.'

'Might I demur that you imagine yourself to be as important inside this surgery as you imagine yourself to be out of it?'

She said furiously, 'A typical male doctor! Doubtless you see women only as sex objects.'

'I should hope so,' I told her. 'If none of us were sex objects on the appropriate occasion the human race would be extinct animals. Might I tell you how utterly bored I am with women who are constantly kicking against the pricks, if you'll pardon that expression. All this nonsense about chairpersons and watchpersons and God's sublime achievement is person, in the next century it'll be a laughable fad, like the Victorians putting skirts round piano legs.'

She grabbed Mrs Radnor's hand, hissed, 'You shall hear more of this,' and slammed the door.

That night saw my retirement dinner. Just Dr Lonelyhearts and Jack Windrush and selected cronies in Soho. I reached home late in a minicab. Sandra was agitated. The newspapers had been telephoning. But I was trying to tell her Windrush's funny story about the tart's hearing aid, and not inclined to pay much attention.

Came the dawn. Horror! I found myself promoted in vilification from the local to the national press. Worthy Sanctuary was obstructed in its merciful work among battered women by callous Dr Gordon, who was unavailable for comment. In my blazing fury at this synthetic disgrace there glowed a tardy realization that people who wrote for newspapers made fork-tongued vipers look as harmless as glow-worms. I wondered if the Queen had read it. I could never have made the speech. It would have been dreadfully uncomfortable for both of us. I thanked God again that I could vanish into retirement, as infamous Nazis into South America.

Jilly appeared unexpectedly at lunchtime.

'I suppose you know that Bertie Taverill's the president of Sanctuary?'

I started, over my cholesterol-free steamed cod.

'But that's like making John Peel patron saint of the Anti-Blood Sports League.'

'Sanctuary has to deal with both men and women, so chose a president who was both.' She hesitated, compressing her lips. 'I don't know what Mr Taverill thinks of your conduct, Daddy, but it won't...won't at all help...my professional career, ug.'

She left the room quickly again.

I took the rest of the day off. I felt we would get on well over a couple of malts, if I met King Lear in the golf club. I went to bed deciding to shirk the surgery for my final day. At 3 a.m. the telephone rang. It was Mr Clew, with violent abdominal pain.

I drove through the icy night. It could not be his habitual couvade, Mrs Clew not being due for a couple of months. The two children were screaming. Mrs Clew was distraught with scarlet-spotted cheeks. Mr Clew was in bed groaning. I examined him and telephoned the General.

'Jilly? It's Daddy. Sorry to rouse you, but I think I've a nasty appendix here.'

'Pop him in an ambulance, go back to bed, and I'll do the rest,' she told me cheerfully.

'I'll have to take the children with me on the demo tomorrow morning,' said Mrs Clew flusteredly.

I asked crossly. 'What demo?'

'Didn't you hear, doctor? The big one Re-Birth is holding outside the General. Oh, I couldn't possibly miss it, even with my husband a patient inside. It'd be like missing my own twenty-first birthday party. There's coaches booked overnight from Manchester, Birmingham and Bath.'

'But you can't hold a demo tomorrow,' I pointed out. 'You'll clash with the Queen.'

'That's the idea,' she told me.

I slept an hour. I supposed I had better go to the surgery. A vanquished soldier must fight till the armistice. I arrived late. In my consulting room was Mrs Radnor, sobbing.

'I didn't mean to do it, honest, doctor.'

'What didn't you mean to do?' I demanded shortly.

'I wouldn't have dreamed of it in a month of Sundays, if it hadn't been for that big lady from the greengrocer's carrying on about women's rights.'

'You've made it up with Fred?'

'No, doctor, I've put him in the General with a fractured skull, from hitting him with a saucepan when he complained at breakfast his bacon was cold. Oh, it's terrible! The police are threatening to shop me, there was reporters everywhere at the hospital for some demo or something, nosy parkers the lot of them, you'd have thought I'd won the pools, and come to think of it, doctor, Fred never hit me in the first place, not even with his elbow by mistake, I caught myself on the kitchen door, but at the time I was that mad at Fred, oh dear, what shall I do, I am a wicked woman.'

'Your husband's not seriously hurt, I hope?' I asked with concern.

'I don't fancy he's too bad, he's being looked after by a lady doctor who was ever so nice to me, and funny thing, she's got the same name as you.'

The telephone rang. Mrs Jenkins had a call from the General.

'That appendix?' I asked Jilly at once. 'Complicated?'

'Don't know, Daddy,' she told me brightly. 'It's still inside.'

I was surprised. 'Really? I thought the surgeons' motto was, "If in doubt, cut it out." '

'I might have done, before I got my Fellowship. But I was suspicious. It wasn't quite right, somehow. Wrong white count, Now he's fine and opening a bottle of champagne.'

'Do your patients pretty well on the surgical wards, don't you?'

'But didn't you hear about Mrs Clew? She arrived for the demonstration this morning, made such an impassioned speech she went into labour, and Bertie Taverill's just delivered her of a little boy. Bertie says he does so wish you GPs would help the consultants by getting the patients' dates right.'

'The couvade!' I exclaimed. 'Mr Clew must be the only case of a father admitted to hospital with labour pains before the mother. Thank God you didn't cut him open.'

Mrs Radnor blew her nose.

'And I hope Bertie Taverill isn't upset about the backlash from my Sanctuary patient?' I asked hastily.

'That's another thing he wanted me to say. He's eternally grateful for the wonderful turn you've done him. He says it's going to make Sanctuary look as ridiculous as the Two Ronnies and a wonderful excuse to resign. He was only talked into heading the paranoic outfit by a Lady someone or other with fibroids.'

'I can't think of any better news to ensure my happy retirement.'

'Oh, and Daddy, Peter Taverill and I are getting married next month. Damn! My bleep. Must go. See you with the Queen.'

The opening ceremony was delightful, freed from the agony of a speech. But... Well... Perhaps my elegant sentences from a patient's record card would have gone better than a half-hour of Basil Barty-Howells, and it would have been a moment worth recalling to my now prospective grandchildren before they took me away to the St Boniface Twilight Home. Still, the Queen smiled at me. I wondered, what *was* she thinking about?

I had only that Friday evening to clear my files from the consulting room to which I should never return. Alone, I wrote my letter of resignation to the Family Practitioner Committee. It was growing late, on a bloody night pissing with rain. I sealed and stamped the envelope. The doorbell rang.

I frowned. Nobody called at the surgery that time of night. Patients telephoned for the partner on call. I opened the front door. Tracey was outside, dripping.

'Doctor,' she said solemnly. 'Come at once.'

'What's up?'

'Mum's having one of her turns.'

I knew the code. Moira was back on the drink.

'How is she?' I asked.

'Seems asleep now, though she's been sick all over.'

I said kindly, 'Really, the other doctor who's on duty tonight is now in charge of Mum's case.'

'Mum told me, if anything happened like this to get you. She said you're the only doctor who can help her.'

I said wearily, 'All right, Tracey, I'll come.'

I went back to the surgery for Mrs Jenkins' red plastic brolly. I saw my letter on the desk. I said, 'I'm buggered if I'll retire.' We left.

The rain drummed fiercely on the top of my opened umbrella. The little girl nestled close to my side and clung to my left arm as she had been bidden. We passed, this odd pair, across the rain-slashed oblong of light that the window cast.

RICHARD GORDON

DOCTOR IN THE HOUSE

Richard Gordon's acceptance into St Swithin's medical school came as no surprise to anyone, least of all him – after all, he had been to public school, played first XV rugby, and his father was, let's face it, 'a St Swithin's man'. Surely he was set for life. It was rather a shock then to discover that, once there, he would actually have to work, and quite hard. Fortunately for Richard Gordon, life proved not to be all dissection and textbooks after all… This hilarious hospital comedy is perfect reading for anyone who's ever wondered exactly what medical students get up to in their training. Just don't read it on your way to the doctor's!

'Uproarious, extremely iconoclastic' – *Evening News*
'A delightful book' – *Sunday Times*

DOCTOR AT SEA

Richard Gordon's life was moving rapidly towards middle-aged lethargy – or so he felt. Employed as an assistant in general practice – the medical equivalent of a poor curate – and having been 'persuaded' that marriage is as much an obligation for a young doctor as celibacy for a priest, Richard sees the rest of his life stretching before him. Losing his nerve, and desperately in need of an antidote, he instead signs on with the Fathom Steamboat Company. What follows is a hilarious tale of nautical diseases and assorted misadventures at sea. Yet he also becomes embroiled in a mystery – what is in the Captain's stomach remedy? And more to the point, what on earth happened to the previous doctor?

'Sheer unadulterated fun' – *Star*

Richard Gordon

Doctor at Large

Dr Richard Gordon's first job after qualifying takes him to St Swithin's where he is enrolled as Junior Casualty House Surgeon. However, some rather unfortunate incidents with Mr Justice Hopwood, as well as one of his patients inexplicably coughing up nuts and bolts, mean that promotion passes him by – and goes instead to Bingham, his odious rival. After a series of disastrous interviews, Gordon cuts his losses and visits a medical employment agency. To his disappointment, all the best jobs have already been snapped up, but he could always turn to general practice…

Doctor Gordon's Casebook

'Well, I see no reason why anyone should expect a doctor to be on call seven days a week, twenty-four hours a day. Considering the sort of risky life your average GP leads, it's not only inhuman but simple-minded to think that a doctor could stay sober that long…'

As Dr Richard Gordon joins the ranks of such world-famous diarists as Samuel Pepys and Fanny Burney, his most intimate thoughts and confessions reveal the life of a GP to be not quite as we might expect… Hilarious, riotous and just a bit too truthful, this is Richard Gordon at his best.

RICHARD GORDON

GREAT MEDICAL DISASTERS

Man's activities have been tainted by disaster ever since the serpent first approached Eve in the garden. And the world of medicine is no exception. In this outrageous and strangely informative book, Richard Gordon explores some of history's more bizarre medical disasters. He creates a catalogue of mishaps including anthrax bombs on Gruinard Island, destroying mosquitoes in Panama, and Mary the cook who, in 1904, inadvertently spread Typhoid across New York State. As the Bible so rightly says, 'He that sinneth before his maker, let him fall into the hands of the physician.'

THE PRIVATE LIFE OF JACK THE RIPPER

In this remarkably shrewd and witty novel, Victorian London is brought to life with a compelling authority. Richard Gordon wonderfully conveys the boisterous, often lusty panorama of life for the very poor – hard, menial work; violence; prostitution; disease. *The Private Life of Jack The Ripper* is a masterly evocation of the practice of medicine in 1888 – the year of Jack the Ripper. It is also a dark and disturbing medical mystery. Why were his victims so silent? And why was there so little blood?

'…horribly entertaining…excitement and suspense buttressed with authentic period atmosphere' – *The Daily Telegraph*

TITLES BY RICHARD GORDON AVAILABLE DIRECT
FROM HOUSE OF STRATUS

Quantity		£	$(US)	$(CAN)	€
	THE CAPTAIN'S TABLE	6.99	11.50	15.99	11.50
	DOCTOR AND SON	6.99	11.50	15.99	11.50
	DOCTOR AT LARGE	6.99	11.50	15.99	11.50
	DOCTOR AT SEA	6.99	11.50	15.99	11.50
	DOCTOR IN CLOVER	6.99	11.50	15.99	11.50
	DOCTOR IN LOVE	6.99	11.50	15.99	11.50
	DOCTOR IN THE HOUSE	6.99	11.50	15.99	11.50
	DOCTOR IN THE NEST	6.99	11.50	15.99	11.50
	DOCTOR IN THE NUDE	6.99	11.50	15.99	11.50
	DOCTOR IN THE SOUP	6.99	11.50	15.99	11.50
	DOCTOR IN THE SWIM	6.99	11.50	15.99	11.50
	DOCTOR ON THE BOIL	6.99	11.50	15.99	11.50
	DOCTOR ON THE BRAIN	6.99	11.50	15.99	11.50
	DOCTOR ON THE JOB	6.99	11.50	15.99	11.50
	DOCTOR ON TOAST	6.99	11.50	15.99	11.50
	DOCTOR'S DAUGHTERS	6.99	11.50	15.99	11.50
	DR GORDON'S CASEBOOK	6.99	11.50	15.99	11.50
	THE FACEMAKER	6.99	11.50	15.99	11.50
	GOOD NEIGHBOURS	6.99	11.50	15.99	11.50

ALL HOUSE OF STRATUS BOOKS ARE AVAILABLE FROM GOOD BOOKSHOPS OR
DIRECT FROM THE PUBLISHER:

Internet: **www.houseofstratus.com** including author interviews, reviews, features.

Email: **sales@houseofstratus.com** please quote author, title and credit card details.

TITLES BY RICHARD GORDON AVAILABLE DIRECT
FROM HOUSE OF STRATUS

Quantity		£	$(US)	$(CAN)	€
	GREAT MEDICAL DISASTERS	6.99	11.50	15.99	11.50
	GREAT MEDICAL MYSTERIES	6.99	11.50	15.99	11.50
	HAPPY FAMILIES	6.99	11.50	15.99	11.50
	INVISIBLE VICTORY	6.99	11.50	15.99	11.50
	LOVE AND SIR LANCELOT	6.99	11.50	15.99	11.50
	NUTS IN MAY	6.99	11.50	15.99	11.50
	THE SUMMER OF SIR LANCELOT	6.99	11.50	15.99	11.50
	SURGEON AT ARMS	6.99	11.50	15.99	11.50
	THE PRIVATE LIFE OF DR CRIPPEN	6.99	11.50	15.99	11.50
	THE PRIVATE LIFE OF FLORENCE NIGHTINGALE	6.99	11.50	15.99	11.50
	THE PRIVATE LIFE OF JACK THE RIPPER	6.99	11.50	15.99	11.50

ALL HOUSE OF STRATUS BOOKS ARE AVAILABLE FROM GOOD BOOKSHOPS OR
DIRECT FROM THE PUBLISHER:

Hotline: UK ONLY: **0800 169 1780**, please quote author, title and credit card details.
INTERNATIONAL: **+44 (0) 20 7494 6400**, please quote author, title and
credit card details.

Send to: **House of Stratus Sales Department**
24c Old Burlington Street
London
W1X 1RL
UK

Please allow for postage costs charged per order plus an amount per book as set out in the tables below:

	£(Sterling)	$(US)	$(CAN)	€(Euros)
Cost per order				
UK	2.00	3.00	4.50	3.30
Europe	3.00	4.50	6.75	5.00
North America	3.00	4.50	6.75	5.00
Rest of World	3.00	4.50	6.75	5.00
Additional cost per book				
UK	0.50	0.75	1.15	0.85
Europe	1.00	1.50	2.30	1.70
North America	2.00	3.00	4.60	3.40
Rest of World	2.50	3.75	5.75	4.25

PLEASE SEND CHEQUE, POSTAL ORDER (STERLING ONLY), EUROCHEQUE, OR INTERNATIONAL MONEY ORDER (PLEASE CIRCLE METHOD OF PAYMENT YOU WISH TO USE)
MAKE PAYABLE TO: STRATUS HOLDINGS plc

Cost of book(s): —————— Example: 3 x books at £6.99 each: £20.97

Cost of order: —————— Example: £2.00 (Delivery to UK address)

Additional cost per book: —————— Example: 3 x £0.50: £1.50

Order total including postage: —————— Example: £24.47

Please tick currency you wish to use and add total amount of order:

☐ £ (Sterling)   ☐ $ (US)   ☐ $ (CAN)   ☐ € (EUROS)

VISA, MASTERCARD, SWITCH, AMEX, SOLO, JCB:

☐☐☐☐☐☐☐☐☐☐☐☐☐☐☐☐☐☐☐☐

Issue number (Switch only):

☐☐☐

Start Date: **Expiry Date:**

☐☐ / ☐☐   ☐☐ / ☐☐

Signature: ————————————

NAME: ————————————————————

ADDRESS: ——————————————————

————————————————————

POSTCODE: —————————

Please allow 28 days for delivery.

Prices subject to change without notice.
Please tick box if you do not wish to receive any additional information. ☐

House of Stratus publishes many other titles in this genre; please check our website (**www.houseofstratus.com**) for more details.